A novel

The Postcard

Tom Connelly

Tom Connelly
The Postcard

ISBN: 9780578068848

Facebook at @tomconnellyauthor
Threads and Instagram @tconnelly11
X @ivyscobie
www.tomconnellyfiction.com

Also by Tom Connelly

The Mansion
Flight Unknown
Zworsky's Children (Book One)
Rise of the Creepers (Book Two)
Charlie One

For Katie

Chapter 1

An Occurrence in the Vestibule

Screeeeeeeech!!!!! Out of nowhere...

I thought it was a car accident, something big. It was nearly three o'clock in the morning as I rested my head back on my hot pillow.

Just when I was about to drift off, I heard tires screeching again. This time, I got out of bed and approached the screened window. The sound came from The Plaza, a few streets from my home. The vehicle purred, as if it was lurking about. Suddenly the car picked up speed—fashionably loud. There was a dramatic pause and then the tires screeched again. The car shifted gears—second, third, fourth—and then sped off as its loud muffler faded into the late suburbia night.

Living near three highways, I've heard a lot of things outside my bedroom window—police sirens, car crashes, brakes locking up, blow outs, loud mufflers, motorcycles, and bravado sounding cars doing donuts in The Plaza parking lot. It didn't bother me, though. Just like the crickets, the jazz of the nighttime highway was nothing more than the white noise of summer nights in upstate New York.

As my attention drifted away from the highway, I noticed how hot and humid it was in my small room. I got back into bed but could not doze off.

Through my window, I could see the three beacon lights on top of the water tower in the distance. I kept staring at the lights as they flashed on and off, on and off, and on and off. For most people, the tower probably meant nothing, as if were an eyesore or a metal giant. But for me, the water tower and its three lights meant something more than just a guide in the sky.

I was a lucky ten-year old kid with commerce practically in the backyard of my home. My neighborhood was constructed around three major highways: Route 9W, Route 32, and behind Route 32, Interstate 84. To top it off, my neighborhood resided directly under a jet path. All three highways and jet path intersected through a little city in upstate New York called Burghville.

Burghville was about an hour drive north of New York City and surrounded by New Jersey, Pennsylvania, and Connecticut, or simply known as the Tri-State area. There was never much to do in Burghville.

We had mountains, the Hudson River, and a great view of West Point. We had fast food chain restaurants, movie theatres and a couple of big malls, if that's what you dug for fun. And if a stranger was passing by, we had a sign that said, WELCOME TO BURGHVILLE, THE CROSSROADS OF THE NORTHEAST. And on those really boring days in the wintertime, when the trees in my neighborhood were bare of their leaves and the banality of life in Burghville was at its summit, I'd stand in my backyard and gawk at the traffic lights as they turned red, yellow and green. I'd stare at the neon signs in The Plaza with its unlit vowels, wondering if there was more to life than strip plazas.

Thursday was the day my mother paid me an allowance of three dollars for my house chores. And every Thursday I made the trip to Woolworth's, located in what I called The Plaza, to spend it all on baseball cards. My route to The Plaza was an easy one. Departing my home, located on Twilight Drive, I crossed through my backyard, leading me to a small patch of woods. Walking through the decomposed leaves from the oak trees, while not brushing up against the poison ivy, I headed southward through my neighbors' yard, who seemed to never mind, and then onto Meadow Street, which ran parallel with Twilight Drive. Passing the second house, I turned right, moving in a southward direction. Approaching The Plaza, I could hear the highway sounds of Route 32. I entered a path that led through another small patch of woods to the highway. Greeting me at the end of the path was a big, rusty sign that read: HUDSON VALLEY PLAZA.

Looking both ways, I crossed Route 32 and entered The Plaza's vast parking lot which I called The Tundra. The Tundra was a sea of black top that led upward to The Plaza. Over the years the color of The Tundra had faded away like an old pair of blue jeans. The yellow lines dividing each parking spot were practically non-existent. And what were the architects of The Plaza thinking, building such a large parking lot? Did they really think we needed this much parking space?

Built in the sixties, The Plaza was designed as an inside/outdoor mall. At one end of The Plaza was JCPenney. At the other was A/C's Hardware, which once was an A&P grocery store. And there was probably another store before the A&P, and so on.

Centered in The Plaza was Woolworth's. Connecting these three stores was a long concrete walkway.

Intermittently along the walkway were open roof areas that contained rectangular shaped gardens of shrubs and small pine trees. Adjacent to the gardens were cherry-colored benches. The gardens were what gave The Plaza its unique look. However, the fancy look of horticulture did nothing to stop the small stores along the walkway from going out of business or moving to another cement world.

The Plaza's business had dwindled over the years. Ever since the new mall opened on the other side of town, people avoided The Plaza. It was apparent that the outdoor malls were not a sensation anymore, at least not in Burghville

Failing to keep up appearances, The Plaza became more and more desolate. If it weren't for JCPenney and Woolworth's, The Plaza probably would cease to exist.

Before I entered Woolworth's, I checked to see if anyone was occupying the red bench. The red bench was my solitude and my home away from home. It was where I opened my baseball cards. It was also where I broke my molar on a Charms grape flavored lollipop. At the bench, I would study the player's stats and history. Some days, I would just watch the few shoppers stroll along the concrete walkway, wondering why they still came to The Plaza.

I saluted the big red capital "W" on the Woolworth's sign and entered the vestibule. Here the candy and gumball machine were strategically positioned for incoming and outgoing customers. There was also the old cigarette machine, with its back facing the outside of the mall's walkway.

As I entered the store, the cool air conditioning gave me goose bumps on my arms. I smelled onions. From the back of the store, I heard the deep fryer sacrificing potatoes. It was 1982, and for some reason, the Woolworth's in Burghville still had their infamous diner.

The store was staffed with mostly old ladies, wearing their red Woolworth's attire. Frank Woolworth not only created the five and dime store, but he was also the first to display store products out on the floor for the shoppers to browse.

The mysticism of Woolworth's fascinated me. I mean, where else could you buy a pair of pants, a top forty album, hard candy, a pet fish, a string of yarn, underwear, socks, a hammer, a monopoly game, and a burger and a milkshake in one place?

I entered the candy aisle and grabbed nine packs of Topps baseball cards. I would have bought the whole box, but three dollars permitted nine.

I stood in line behind a woman and her son. Judging by the size of the clothes in the woman's red basket, the clothes were for him. He seemed to be the same age as me. For some unknown reason he would not look at me; he was probably embarrassed, and I don't blame him. I would have felt weird if one of my classmates knew I bought clothes from Woolworth's. For a ten-year-old boy, Woolworth's meant buying candy, records, comics and baseball cards—not clothes! However, I did not know this kid, and he did not know me. He was safe whether he knew it or not.

I turned my eyes to the slug lines on the house and gardening magazines, wondering who would read this crap. There was another scream from the deep fryer, freeing me from my Woolworth's trance.

I turned to see the boy and his mother exiting the store. I placed the nine packs on the counter and looked up at the clerk. The clerk's name tag said LORETTA, and she smelled like cigarettes.

"You sure like baseball," she rasped. "I see you here each Thursday. You ever think about saving your money?"

She rang up my total for the cards.

"I'm trying to collect every card in the eighty-one series."

"But it's 1982?"

I smiled and then handed her my three dollars.

"At least you don't spend it on cigarettes, like those jackals out there." She nodded toward the window. It was James Le-Bleau and a couple of his cronies, sitting on my favorite bench. They were all teenagers and lived in the same neighborhood as mine. Even on that hot summer day, in the Tri-State area, they wore their jean jackets and sun absorbing black pants.

LeBleau was the leader of his crew. He was known for his frequent fights and his unsung demeanor. I watched one of Le-Bleau's friends hand him a couple of dollars. He then proceeded into the store. His black wavy hair bounced firmly on his shoulders as he strolled up to the counter. He was wearing a new shirt. The shirt was as black as space. In the middle of the abyss was a picture of a living skeleton. The "skeleton man" had eyes and long hair and was wielding an ax. Blood dripped from the blade of the ax, as if he just chopped his victim into bits and pieces. Underneath it read KILLERS. Above the skeleton man, in strange red lettering, read IRON MAIDEN.

"Yo, Loretta. Eight quarters," LeBleau barked as he dropped a couple of crumbled dollar bills onto the counter.

"Your parents know you smoke?" Loretta asked sternly.

LeBleau tapped the counter with his index finger. "Just give me the quarters, will ya?"

She opened the register. And on that cue, I grabbed my plastic Woolworth's shopping bag full of baseball cards and headed toward the vestibule.

"You rock, Loretta," LeBleau said as he followed behind me.

As I pushed open the door and entered the vestibule, I could feel his eyes on my back. He had curious eyes, eyes that probably had never shed a tear, eyes as dry as the Mojave Desert. As I held the door for him, he asked jokingly, "Yo, Bailey. What you got in the bag? Marijuana?"

As I turned toward him, I dropped my bag of cards. LeBleau swiped it from the floor like a dirty seagull. He looked inside of it. "Oh shit, you like baseball?"

I nodded a "yes."

"Who's your favorite player?"

"Reggie Jackson," I said.

LeBleau handed me back my bag and began depositing the quarters into the coin slot of the cigarette machine.

"What about you? Who's your favorite player?"

"I don't like watching baseball. Too fucking slow," Le-Bleau said, as if he had no soul.

I couldn't keep my eyes off of his strange shirt. I wanted to know where he got it and ask him who the hell is Iron Maiden.

LeBleau pulled the lever for his cigarettes.

Nothing happened.

He pulled the lever again.

Nothing.

And then he punched the machine.

"Fucker ate my quarters!" He turned to me. "You got any quarters, Bailey?"

"No."

"Shit." LeBleau huffed and puffed as he ran his hand through his long and wavy black hair. He punched the tobacco machine again. "Don't ever smoke, Bailey."

LeBleau punched the machine for the third time as the noise echoed in the vestibule. Just then, the quarters fell to whatever part of the machine they were supposed to fall to. He smiled and pulled the lever as a pack of Marlboros dropped down. He pointed his index finger at me, the same one he vehemently tapped on Loretta's counter with, and said, "Don't smoke, Bailey, or I'll fuck you up." He then grabbed his unlucky cigarettes from the slot and headed back to his crew.

I sat at another bench in a different section of The Plaza and opened all nine packs of cards. Each pack contained a stick of pink gum. This wasn't special baseball gum. No, it was not made by the great players who resided in these fantastic baseball packs. It was simply pink, hard, and as stale as a bingo game. It was like chewing the morning paper. Things could be worse, I guess.

Every nine years Topps Baseball Card Company included an extra card called "In Action." This series of cards featured the all-star players from the previous season. I had collected all the In Action players from the 1981 season, except for Reggie Jackson.

If you were a Yankees fan in the late seventies, you knew Reggie was called "Mr. October." He was given this name after hitting three home runs in the sixth game of the 1977 World Series. I checked all nine packs and still no sign of Mr. October.

As I double checked the cards, I saw that I got another George Brett (the third baseman of the Kansas City Royals). I must have had ten copies of George. I packaged all the bubble gum tainted cards back into my Woolworth's bag and headed off.

As I walked along The Tundra, I noticed the sun was caressing the western horizon.

My father had once told me that when the streetlights go on, I must be home or miss dinner. I didn't know any other ten-year olds who were so self-sufficient. I wanted to go home anyway, so I could watch the ball game in the air conditioned T.V. room.

Walking halfway across The Tundra, I heard rock music. I looked back and spotted LeBleau holding a radio as he and his crew walked toward the water tower. They sang along—more like shouted. I saw one of his friends banging his head to the beat. The music was fast and hard. I heard someone call this music "metal."

I kind of liked it.

Chapter 2

Look Both Ways

On my eleventh birthday my parents bought me a bicycle. The color of the bike was wine red. Clipped in between the tire spokes were bright orange reflectors. Declared in silver lettering on the bike's frame was the name: THE EXPLORER. I couldn't take stock in the name. I had just turned eleven and had to be home when the streetlights flicked on. However, I would no longer walk to The Plaza. My mother thought it was dangerous for me to ride my bike along Route 32. My father, on the other hand, knew I was getting older and that I should learn responsibility. And as long as I walked my bike across Route 32, my parents said it would not be an issue.

With the added twenty bucks that my father had secretly given me, I peddled out of my driveway and onto Twilight Drive. It was another hot and humid day as I road along. And the humid breeze did nothing to cool me down. I made a right turn on Powell Drive, which led directly to Route 32. Reaching Route 32, I walked my bike across the highway. Once I reached the entrance of The Tundra, I hopped back onto the seat and peddled to the top and parked my bike outside of Woolworth's.

As I entered the store, the air conditioning cooled my blood. I looked up at the clock above the entrance; the duration of the trip took me ten minutes. By foot, it would have taken me at least twenty minutes or more. I headed straight to the candy aisle and grabbed, not nine, but ten packs of Topps baseball cards.

As I stood in line to pay for the cards, I was surprised to see a different person working. Then I remembered Loretta did not work on Saturdays. I wondered what Loretta did on her days off. Did she have grandchildren? Maybe her kids are older versions of James LeBleau.

As I exited the store, I was happy to see no sign of LeBleau and his cronies sitting on my bench. Just as I was about to sit, I noticed that someone had engraved a message into the cherry-colored wood of the bench. It was shaped like a heart. Inside the heart it read: LISA & JAMES

It couldn't be. Not James LeBleau! He was too tough for girls. Who was Lisa? And did she have enough emotions to like or even love LeBleau?

Could James LeBleau love someone?

I placed my bag over the engraved message and ripped through nine packs of cards. There was still no sign of my Reggie Jackson card. Now it was time for number ten. I opened the pack and shuffled through a few cards. And there it was! Reggie Jackson in pinstripes! The picture captured Reggie at bat, swinging at a pitch. And judging by his expression, he probably got a hit, maybe a double or a triple, maybe even a homerun. Or maybe he struck out? Who knows? One thing that was true: the Yankees sucked in 1982, and worst, Reggie had been traded to the California Angels. But I completed the In Action series, and it was time to go home and check in the cards. I hopped onto the seat of The Explorer and peddled off.

As I reached the mouth of The Tundra, I looked to the water tower in the distance. Throttling the rubber handlebars, I slowly rode toward the tower. I stopped at A/C's Hardware store. From here, The Tundra led upward to the tower. It was the highest point and the most desolate section of The Plaza. In the winter, the plows used this slice of The Tundra to store huge piles of snow that looked like something from Antarctica. I decided to wrestle the August sunrays and ride to the top.

My shirt was soaked in sweat and my legs ached as I rode closer and closer to the tower.

Halfway, I jumped off my bike to catch my breath. *The hell with this*, I thought. I walked the rest of the way.

The sounds of trucks and cars from Interstate 84, which had been faint from my bedroom window, were now loud and aggressive. I sat on the hot pavement and used my white T-shirt to wipe the salty sweat from my face. At the bottom of the hill, I saw cars zoom along Route 32. In the far distance, I saw the trees that buried my neighborhood from the busy highways.

I looked up at the white tower, which stood like a giant creature with its rusty freckles. The creature's four legs regally held its head high into the hazy summer sky.

Running down the middle of the tower was a large intestinal pipe, penetrating the ground like an umbilical cord. Small rods connected each leg in a spider-web like fashion—just to give it some pizzazz. Pasted to the tower's left back leg was a ladder, leading to its outer head.

On each side of the rim were the beacon lights, like red eyeballs, which I could see forever winking at me through my bedroom window.

Around the rim of its belly was a walkway for the maintenance workers, which marked trouble for suburban teens. To prevent curious teens from the creature's luxurious view of the Hudson Valley, a ten-foot sheet of metal was locked into the first ten steps of the ladder. According to the legend, there was a reason why this metal sheet was inserted over the ladder.

One fall night, two kids, high on weed, had decided to immortalize their temporary existence onto the barrel of the water tower. Their names were Roland and Malcolm. I didn't know their last names.

Lungs full of pot and jacket pockets containing cans of spray paint, Roland and Malcolm climbed to the top of the tower. They sat on the edge of the walkway with their legs dangling in the atmosphere. They laughed at the passing traffic as they smoked more weed. No need to worry when you were seventeen.

When the roll of weed was gone, they painted: CLASS OF 75. As they inked the big 75, they didn't expect the fumes from the spray paint to make them sleepy. Or maybe it was drugs. With their hands covered with red paint and their lungs now filled with marijuana, hydrocarbons and tar, Roland and Malcolm passed out on the rim.

They awoke an hour later.

And to their dismay, the big high had left them. And like the unexpected quarterback sneak, reality got first down. They were now hungry and cold. Too scared to climb down the ladder, there was only one way for them to call for help. Using the beacon lights as a guide, they slowly moved around the tower's rim. Opposite of the CLASS OF 75, they spray painted: HELP, 2 KIDS TRAPPED. But nighttime can skew the mind. And with the water tower curving, instead of a nice and flat canvas, their S.O.S. said: HEL P KID ST RAP PED

The cry for help now looked like the logo for a rap artist. In a desperate cry for help, one of them threw a spray can at the passing traffic on Interstate 84, hoping to catch someone's attention. The can landed in the back of a cattle rig, arousing a calf with a MOO.

It was not until the early morning, bladders full, they would be rescued.

Not sure if it was Roland or Malcolm, but one of them urinated off the rim of the tower. Whoever it was, they were lucky, because that was the day the maintenance worker came to inspect the tower.

A drizzle fell upon the maintenance man. The sprinkle smelled funny, and sort of burned a bit. The man looked for gray clouds, but instead saw a teenager pissing off the side of the water tower. The fire department arrived and rescued the kids. The police were there too, waiting to take them away. A week later, CLASS OF 75 and HEL P KID ST RAP PED was painted over. And worst of all, they did not graduate until 1976.

I stretched out on the grassy area near one of the tower's legs and stared up at the slow passing clouds. Listening to the noise of the highway, I felt drowsy. I closed my eyes and felt a cool breeze against my body.

In the distance, I heard an airliner approaching. As the noise of the plane grew louder, I slowly opened my eyes to see, not an airliner, but the mammoth military C-5 flying over the barrel of the tower. I stood and was shocked to see the streetlights were on. The sun was buried in the horizon line. Dinner was getting cold, and Dad's blood was probably getting hot. I couldn't believe I had fallen asleep. I jumped on my bike and quickly rode off.

I slowed down as I reached Route 32. I jumped off my bike and began to walk along the highway. It was about two hundred yards to Powell Street. I felt my back getting sweaty. The highway was slow.

I looked both ways and then hopped onto my bike.

I began cutting diagonally across the highway.

Suddenly, I heard an engine purring behind me. From the corner of my left eye, I saw the grill of a car.

And the car did not stop, nor did the driver blow its horn.

The front of the car clipped my back tire, throwing me and The Explorer into the middle of the highway. I landed on top of my left arm, while my bag of baseball cards splattered over Route 32 like a yoke from a broken egg.

Dazed, I looked up and saw the car had pulled over. I waited. I waited. And I waited. No one got out.

There was a sudden gust of wind as my Woolworth's bag danced in the distance. A baseball card flipped forward, nudging my bloody arm. It was Bucky Dent, the shortstop for the Yankees. He was a hero to many New Yorkers in 1978, and the arch enemy of all Boston Red Sox fans. His homerun in the playoff game against the Red Sox landed the Yankees into the 1978 World Series.

Someone shouted in the distance. "Bailey! Bailey! Are you okay?"

The voice sounded familiar.

I looked up and saw James LeBleau running toward me from Powel Street.

The car that hit me drove off.

LeBleau yelled to the driver. "Where you going, asshole?"

Reaching me, and out of breath, Lebleau asked, "Can you walk?"

I tried but couldn't stand. "I think I broke my arm."

"Don't move," he said. LeBleau bent down and slowly picked me up, and he carried me across the street. He was wearing his Iron Maiden shirt, and he smelled like cigarettes. He placed me onto the side of the highway. I looked at the blood dripping from the ax on his shirt, then I looked at my left arm. I suddenly felt sick.

"I'm gonna call an ambulance," LeBleau said, and he ran off to The Plaza.

I looked at the water tower in the distance and thought about those two kids. Cars were slowing down to look at me.

Some saw the bike and made the connection. One car stopped as a man dressed in a fancy business suit got out.

"What happened?"

"Car hit me," I said.

Fancy Suit Man looked to see if the car that had hit me was still around.

"Don't bother. He took off," I said.

Another car pulled over as a chubby fellow quickly got out. He smelled like garlic. "What the hell happened?" he asked.

"Hit and run," Fancy Suit Guy said.

"Jesus!"

Garlic Man looked at my bike. "I better move the bike." He jogged into the middle of the highway as his pants hung low off his big butt. He picked up The Explorer and carried it across the road, as if it was a dead animal. I watched the chain hang off the back tire, as if the bike had been gutted by a hunter. After he placed it onto the side of the road, he pulled up his pants.

I noticed the bike's handlebars were twisted. The orange reflector was missing.

I looked and saw more of my baseball cards boogying along the highway. One of them was my Reggie Jackson card.

"I'll call an ambulance," Garlic Man said with shortness of breath.

"Someone already did," I said.

"Who?" the Fancy Suit Guy asked.

"Him," I said, pointing toward The Plaza.

Both men saw James LeBleau, the metal head who hated cigarette machines, running back from The Plaza.

My left arm was in a cast for the rest of the summer. I once saw this kid at school who had a cast on his leg, which was blanketed with writing. I couldn't read what was written on it, but it looked kind of cool. So I asked one of the nurses who took care of me in the emergency room to write a message on mine. She did, and wrote: GET BETTER, JIMMY. My brother wrote: THE HEALTH SYSTEM IN AMERICA IS AT PAR WITH THE BURGER KINGS' MEN'S ROOM. My brother worked one week at the local Burger King and was fired for telling the patrons that meat was the main factor for heart disease. Not sure what all that had to do with the health care system. My older sister wrote, hopefully with no pun intended: BREAK AN ARM, BROTHER. Mom wrote: HANG TOUGH. And Dad simply wrote: GET WELL. Their messages were all boring.

The driver who knocked me off my bike was not caught by the police. The police had said the newspaper article about my accident would help with the investigation. The article appeared the day after the accident. Here's what some of it said:

James Bailey, who just turned eleven yesterday, was involved with a hit and run. While crossing Route 32 on his bicycle, James was knocked into the middle of the highway by a passing car. The driver of the car stopped, but then proceeded to drive away while James lay hurt in the middle of a busy highway. Coming to James' aid was seventeen year old James LeBleau. My Trans Am was in the shop, getting new brakes. I needed some smokes. As I was walking to the Woolworth's, I heard a car jam on its brakes, *Lebleau said. James yelled to the driver in the car, but the driver did not respond. The green Plymouth then sped off.* I saw Bailey in the middle of the road. I ran over to Bailey, picked him up and carried him off to the side of the highway.

I flirted with the idea of gluing the newspaper clipping over the writing on my cast, but then decided to clip it on my bedroom wall—right next to my Reggie Jackson poster.

It was Thursday, and summer was almost over. My arm was no longer in a sling, but I was still wearing a small cast. Although I could not do my chores, my mother still gave me three dollars. And she gave me permission to walk to The Plaza. My father had fixed The Explorer. However, with one functioning arm, biking to The Plaza would be treacherous and could result in two broken arms. Cutting through the woods and banging into tree branches was unsafe, so I took the long route.

Walking along Twilight Drive, I heard a boisterous car growing behind me. As I reached Powel Drive, the sound of the car continued to grow. I turned toward the sound and saw a black Trans Am approaching. The car stopped alongside me as the engine rumbled like an old washing machine. It was James LeBleau. He shouted, "Get in."

I opened the door with my right hand and slowly positioned myself into the front seat. I slammed the heavy door as we drove off.

The car was unlike LeBleau. The floor was clear of the normal straw wrappers, cigarette boxes, pennies, pebbles, aspirin, hair, receipts, and empty cassette cases. Hanging from the rearview mirror was a skull.

As the car picked up speed, the vibration from the muffler. As I held the arm of the door handle with my right hand, I noticed that LeBleau was not wearing his seat belt.

"Where are you going?" he asked.

"The Plaza."

"Let me guess, the big W?"

I had never heard anyone call Woolworth's "The big W." It sounded cool. And from that point on, I would call it that.

"You like that store, huh?" he said.

"I get my baseball cards there."

I continued to size up the interior of the car. "This is nice," I said.

"Been in the shop for a while. But I just got it back the other day."

We stopped at Route 32 as the car anxiously rumbled. "So, you like collecting ball cards."

Before I could respond, he added, "Open the glove compartment."

I opened it and saw a crumpled brown bag.

"Grab it," LeBleau said.

I grabbed the bag. "What's this?"

"Look inside."

I opened it and saw a bunch of baseball cards. Most of them were dirty; some had scratches.

"I picked up as many as I could find," he said. "I used to collect ball cards when I was younger."

I reached into the bag and grabbed a card. It was George Brett of the Kansas City Royals, of all players.

"Why?" I asked.

He did not respond.

"Thanks," I said.

"I hope they catch that fucker and put his dick in a rusty vice."

The volume on the radio was low, but I knew he was listening to Iron Maiden.

"Is this Iron Maiden?"

He smiled. "You like Iron Maiden?"

"They sound cool."

"Hell yeah! It's fucking Maiden!" He increased the volume. The song was called "Running Free." The music was mean and aggressive. I don't know why but it connected with me. I nodded my head to the beat as we pulled into The Tundra. The engine revved as LeBleau shifted gears.

"Hold on Bailey."

LeBleau punched the gas as the tires ripped into The Tundra's skin; a sound that I knew all too well. I laughed as we sped to the entrance to The Plaza.

LeBleau turned down the radio.

Through the window, I saw the big red "W" on the Woolworth's sign. I held out my right hand to him. "Thanks for the ride and for my cards."

He shook it and said, "No problem."

Before I got out of the car, I looked at the water tower in the distance for a few seconds. I then turned to him and said, "And thanks for helping me out."

Before I stepped out, he said, "Hey, that's some crazy writing on your cast."

I looked back at him. "You want to write something on it?"

James grabbed a pen out of the glove compartment.

"Write whatever you want," I said.

And he did.

He simply wrote: LOOK BOTH WAYS.

I entered the big W and headed straight for the candy aisle. I reached down and grabbed a pack of baseball cards. As I held the pack in my hand, I started to hum the song, "Running Free." The song was stuck in my head. I held the pack of cards in my hand for a moment. I placed the pack back into the box and then walked to the music section.

I had bought a few 45's here, mostly Top 40 stuff, but never anything metal. I searched through the "I" section and came across two Iron Maiden LPs.

One was the obvious *Killers* album, which had the infamous picture of the skeleton man holding the bloody ax. I held up the LP to examine the cover. The artwork showed plenty of details. The artist chose to show only the victim's hands holding the skeleton man's shirt. I assume the man fell to the ground after being bludgeoned by the skeleton man. What an intense album cover! And it was for sale at The Big W!

There was one other Iron Maiden LP simply called *Iron Maiden*. It had that same skeleton man on it. But this time the man was standing under a city streetlight. It was nighttime and his hair was spiked high, as if he saw the devil himself.

I flipped the back of it and read that "Running Free" was one of the songs on the album. The price tag on the album said $7.99. I had the three dollars my mother gave me, and some money left over from my birthday. But did I have enough guts to buy it?

As I walked to the register, I saw Loretta was working. She was shocked to see my left arm in a cast. "My God! What happened?"

"I got hit by a car on my bike."

"You were the boy who got hit by the car?"

"Yes," I said.

"I read about you in the paper. I hope they catch the driver."

I felt weird as I placed the Iron Maiden record on the checkout counter. Strangely, Loretta didn't seem surprised by it. She simply asked, "No baseball cards?"

"Not today," I said.

That afternoon I walked home with Iron Maiden's first album—my first metal record. No, I did not buy any baseball cards that day. In fact, I never bought a pack of baseball cards again.

Chapter 3

Last Paycheck

In the summer of 1990, the rain had decided not to visit Burghville. For many years the weathermen had kept records of hot summers, and they had said that 1990 was the warmest summer so far. There was plenty of evidence to show: green lawns had turned potato brown, old dogs panted for dear life, and air conditioners filled the air with white noise. Most people headed to the indoor malls to escape the heat, but me, Anthony Russo and Stanley Foster, whom we called "Handsome," had preferred the old Plaza.

In three days, I would be taking a plane to attend film school out west, leaving Burghville, my friends and family behind. I knew nothing about what was happening or was going to happen in Burghville. The only event to look forward to was the rain, and even that was uncertain.

We were out of cigarettes.

And nobody liked going into the big W to get change to buy smokes out of the machine. Russo did it last time, so it was either me or Handsome to make the tobacco purchase. Russo stretched out his arms and made a fist with his right hand. He had a better plan; he always had a better plan.

"I got an idea! Whoever grunts, buys!" Russo declared.

"What?" I asked.

"I'll punch you both in the arm. Whoever cries, buys."

Handsome and I shrugged as we looked at each other. We then faced sideways toward Russo. I prayed that he would choose my right arm. I never told them about my bicycle mishap. For some reason, I couldn't talk to my friends about the accident.

"Ready?" Russo asked.

Russo was a drummer. And like all drummers, he had strong forearms.

Anthony Russo was seventeen years of age and played drums for a speed metal band called Dead and Gone. They were a popular band in Burghville. Or, as someone once pejoratively called them, "a promising local band." They had shows booked almost every other weekend and occasionally would open for a national act.

Russo had made a name for himself when the first Dead and Gone recording called *No Unsolution* had circulated around town. Local percussionists were dazzled by his drumming style. Many of them had asked him questions about a certain drum roll or a beat in a song. Russo said he had no tricks when it came to creating a drum pattern. He just listened to the song, figured out the timing and played the beat. It was that simple. However, he believed drumming should complement the song; to overplay would be disrespecting the tune.

Russo schooled himself by listening to his favorite metal albums. He once told me he would jerk up the volume from his radio and play along with the tune. Sometimes I would hear him tapping, and knew, in his mind, he was listening to a song, trying to figure out the drum beat.

I came to know the great Russo in the tenth grade. It was Sequential Math, a class that would serve no meaning or purpose in my life.

On the first day of class, Russo had sat in the back, right next to the windows—a place with the most proximity to freedom. He wore a black rock shirt under his unbuttoned blue flannel. I could not see the name of the band on the shirt. But when the bell rang, he took off his flannel, revealing the shirt. I had never seen such menacing artwork on a piece of clothing. At the bottom of the shirt were decapitated human heads floating in pools of blood, and in the background were lifeless bodies hanging upside down. Above all this chaos, read the band name SLAYER. Below the name, it read REIGN IN BLOOD. Even stranger, Russo wore a gold crucifix around his neck. Russo was an Italian American and catholic. He was baptized at Saint Mary's church in Burghville, the same church where he had made his communion and confirmation. Russo came from a large family. He had three older brothers and an older sister. He told me shouting and arguing was a way of life for him. His family owned a cement and gravel company.

Like many Italian immigrants, Russo's grandparents were hard workers who came to build a life in the good old U.S.A. His grandparents passed on this work ethic to Russo's dad, and somehow it led to Russo being the best metal drummer in Burghville.

After class, I had asked Russo about Slayer. Russo smiled as he retrieved his Walkman from his book bag that contained no books. He put the headphones over my ears and hit play as the sound of Slayer entered my brain. The drumming was incredible, the guitar riffs were sickly fast, and the vocals were chaotic. It was the best album I had ever heard.

Up until that point, I had purchased all the Iron Maiden records; I had Queensryche, Motley Crue, Twisted Sister, Scorpions, AC/DC and many others. Before Slayer, the heaviest band I had heard was Metallica.

But Slayer was in a class of music called "thrash" or "death metal," depending on where you stood. It was a new style of metal music that was making waves in America in the late eighties. Most fans of thrash and death metal, at least the ones I knew, did not care for bands like Poison, White Lion and

Great White; they called it "poser music" or "shit rock." For the record, I never called any one a poser for the music they liked. And I didn't care about labels. I'd give any band a shot regardless of their genre. But Slayer was something else. And so was Russo.

Russo cocked back his arm. He smiled at Handsome and then punched his arm. Handsome puckered his lips, as if he just sucked twenty lemons. Russo looked at me with an inimical smile. He punched my bad arm. I tried to hold back the pain, but the sting was slicing into me like a stomach cramp.

"Son of a bitch!"

As I held my arm in agony, Russo and Handsome laughed like local Friday night drunks.

"Here you go, Bailey," Russo said as he pounded two dollars into my hand.

Handsome snapped his fingers. "Now get those cigarettes."

I walked through the door of the big W. As usual, the air conditioning was fantastic. With that high ceiling, it must cost them tons of money to keep this joint cool. I approached Loretta, who still worked the register, and asked for change. I remembered how she had scolded LeBleau for buying cigarettes. But she never said a word to me.

I jingled the quarters in my hand and entered the vestibule. The cigarette machine was still in its same location, with its same late seventies Kools and Marlboro logos. And who could forget the dents created by LeBleau's teenage rage. I popped the quarters into the slot and pulled the lever. I packed the cigarettes on the palm of my hand, and then walked out of the big W.

"Hi, Jimmy," a girl's voice said sweetly.

Seeing Stacey Polanski, and her new punk rock/hardcore haircut, sitting on Handsome's lap, I sensed trouble.

I opened the cigarette pack and blew the tobacco off the top of the butts. I grabbed one and tossed the pack to Russo.

"Got one for me?" Stacey asked Russo.

"Get your own pack, Sergeant SS," Russo said.

Russo's feet were pounding on the cement like a mini marching band; he was touching up on his double bass drum, a drum technique big with thrash bands.

"Fuck you, and quit the Nazi semantics," she said.

Russo did a triplet with his feet, a roll on his lap, and finished it with a pat on Stacey's shaved head.

"It's stupid metal heads like yourself that give the scene a bad rep," she said.

"The scene?" Russo mimicked in a women's voice.

"Yeah, that's what they call it in the city."

"That's fucking retarded," Russo said.

Russo stuck a cigarette in his mouth and tossed the pack to Handsome.

"You're not going to share one with me?" Stacey asked Handsome.

"No, we are not going to share one with you," Russo said.

Stacey snapped. "I wasn't talking to you, Reaganite!"

It was a site to behold, seeing a girl sitting on Handsome's lap. As far as I knew, this was his first time.

"Here you go," Handsome said, handing Stacey a cigarette.

"Didn't those twisted nuns teach you anything in that school?" Russo asked jokingly.

Sure, cigarettes cause cancer. But they also cause hardship amongst friends who don't have jobs.

Stacey lit her cigarette and said to Russo, "You should cut your hair short. You might get a girlfriend."

Russo stood and defensively said, "Like your hair? No thank you!"

She took a big drag of her cigarette and blew a carbon dioxide ring in my face. "You're damp today, James."

Stacey was a metal chick who recently found the hardcore scene.

Like punk rock, hardcore was a form of underground music. But the music was more aggressive. Most hardcore bands were unknown to the mainstream world of music. They had little or no airplay on the radio. And you never saw a hardcore band on MTV. At the time, most major record companies stayed away from this style of music. If a hardcore band did release a record, it was through an independent label, and the sound quality of the record was usually shit. But that didn't matter to the fans; a good sound production was a sign of selling out, so the shittier the sound, the better. Most kids into hardcore hated metal and thrash. In a nutshell, the thrash crowd hated the hair metal crowd, and the hardcore and punk crowd hated them all.

But there was only a small crowd who followed the hardcore scene in Burghville, and Stacey was now a part of it. Her once long beautiful red hair was now shaved. But her bangs were long, and she died them blonde. She wore a white T-shirt that read F.U. They were a local hardcore band, and she was dating the lead singer. The shirt hung over her jean shorts, while her fishnet stockings clenched tight to her legs. And Handsome couldn't keep his eyes off of them.

"Well, it's time for me to leave this party," I said.

"Where are you going, Bailey?" Russo asked.

"Pick up my last paycheck."

"How could I forget, college man is departing on Monday," Stacey said sarcastically.

"Don't be such a femme fatale," I said.

Stacey winked at me as she took another drag of her free cigarette.

"Are you coming back tonight?" Handsome asked.

"Sure," I said.

My car was parked in The Tundra. Actually, it was my mother's. Before I got into the four wheeled machine, I turned and saw Stacey's ass had left Handsome's lap. Handsome had the worst luck.

Handsome was a little over six feet tall, a bit lanky. He once had a bad case of zits. You can still see some of the scars on his face from picking at them.

I remember first meeting him and listening to his long talks about forming a metal band. Yet he did not know what instrument he wanted to play. He tried drums for a while, then guitar, and even dabbled with singing. But his family objected to his metal fantasies. And they vehemently would not allow him to grow his hair long. They were super religious and viewed metal music as devil's music.

But Handsome would not surrender his dreams. Metal was his release; it was his umbilical cord into an imaginary place only he could occupy. But he never formed a band.

I met him through Russo. He was one of the many students who had graduated from catholic school to attend four years of public high school. When I first met him, he tried to get me into these metal bands I'd never heard of. A lot of them I didn't like. I think he wanted to be a trendsetter. He also liked to pick a fight. If you disagreed with his opinion, he'd talk to you until your face turned sour. One day he told Russo that Dave Lombardo—the drummer for Slayer—was sloppy. He also added that Slayer was over-hyped. Russo responded by kicking him in the groin. And Handsome never talked about drummers again with Russo. We respected Handsome for who he was. He was our knucklehead, and we loved him like no other.

As I opened the door to my mother's red 1987 Nissan Sentra, a mirage of heat blasted out of the car. The Sentra had no air conditioner, no CD player, no RPM gauge, no power steering, and, frankly, no gas. However, it did have an ashtray, a cigarette lighter, cigarette burns on the seat, and plenty of miles to fill its mind with candid memories. As I drove off, I was hoping that Handsome was not falling for Stacey.

It had been one week since I counted empty bottles and cans at Jack's Stack glorious redemption center. Jack's Stack was the only beer and soda wholesaler in Burghville. Jack Shea, the owner of the Stack, once told me how he came up with the idea to open a beer and beverage store: "When America is down, people drink, and when America is happy, people drink." And here's why I decided to work at Jack's Stack: "When you are not old enough to drink, get a job at a beer store." Counting empties at Jack's was a sought-after job. Your paycheck was small, but your choice of beverage was vast. But all good things must come to an end, and so it was time for me to say goodbye to Jack and his wonderful stack.

I entered the store and saw Mr. Shea with his arms crossed intensely. His blue eyes were focused on the small television.

Mr. Shea was a short and thin fellow. His salt and pepper hair was thick around the lower part of his scalp, but on top he had lost the war. To show his defeat with top baldness, he styled some of the hairs from the side of his scalp across the empty terrain. And laughing was the head of the black comb that vacationed in the right back pocket of his blue jeans.

When Mr. Shea was angry (usually a lot) his scalp would turn red, and the few pieces of hair used to subterfuge his baldness would fall in front of his face.

I heard the crack of a bat from the small television. The Yankees were playing the Red Sox. But I didn't care. Baseball had come and gone with me. I had no idea what the Yankees status was that year and could care less. I watched The Yankees during the shit years. Yogi Berra as a manager, then back to Billy Martin, then Lou Penella. Steinberger pissed off Yogi, pissed me off, pissed off New Yorkers. It was 1990, and I was still pessimistic.

Mr. Shea saw me grabbing a can of orange soda from the cooler and asked, "What do you want, Jimmy?" Shea asked.

"Pick up my paycheck."

"I'll cut your check right after this horrible inning."

"I'm gonna head over to the redemption center," I said.

"Tell your friend back there to lower the radio," he yelled.

I knew why Jack was in a bad mood—and it was not because of the Yankees.

As I entered the redemption center, Milky, my childhood friend and co-worker, was sitting on top of a half pallet of Budweiser, rubbing his chiseled chin, reading the Spectrum section of the local newspaper.

When Milky rubbed his chin, it usually meant he was perturbed by something.

Milky's real name was Robert Mitchell. He got his name because he liked to eat Milky Way candy bars. He kept a tab of all the cavities he had filled (seventeen and counting) and carelessly said that he did not fear Novocaine injections.

"Anything good in the paper?" I asked.

Milky smacked the paper with his right hand and said, "I can't believe Cry Baby is playing The Cathedral. Those shit rock fuckers are headlining their own show!"

Milky was the guitarist for Russo's band. I was comfortable saying that Milky had talent for almost everything and could do anything he wanted. I knew him the longest out of all my friends. We first met in the lovely and innocent world called kindergarten. But our friendship blossomed in the tyrannical world of high school. I had introduced Milky to Russo in the tenth grade. Russo was looking to form a speed metal band. I knew Milky could play guitar, but I was unaware of how talented he was on the six-string machine. He was also ripe in the field of songwriting, particularly in the realm of speed metal. Milky could be and do anything he wished. And with all that talent, he declined admission to a four-year college in New England and, instead, chose to go to community college so he could continue to play with Dead and Gone. Russo should be glad. If Milky left the band, Dead and Gone would become the victim of its own name.

Milky crumpled the paper and said, "Jimmy, it's all downhill when the local hair bands are headlining shows at The Cathedral. What's the world coming to? I mean, it's bad enough we have to deal with their videos on Headbangers Ball."

The Cathedral was the hottest venue for a local band to play in the Hudson Valley. It was small, but it had atmosphere. At least four hundred people could cram into its icky space. Dead and Gone got a headlining show this past spring and brought in three hundred people—the biggest draw for a band still in high school. By chance, John Spiro, a local writer and editor of the Spectrum section, was at the show. I had heard the reason Spiro showed up was because he thought Dead and

Gone were a jazz fusion band. Even though Spiro hated speed metal, he thought Dead and Gone were great. He particularly liked Milky's guitar playing. Spiro had a one-hour radio show on the classic rock station devoted to the local music scene. He invited Milky for a brief interview. I quickly found out that there was one thing Milky was not good at.

Here's how it went:

SPIRO

I have seen probably the best young guitarist in the Hudson Valley. He is seventeen years old, and his name is Robert Mitchell, but he goes by the name "Milky." Milky plays for a metal band called Dead and Gone, an up-and-coming band in the upstate area. Most teenage garage bands focus on doing cover tunes from their favorite bands. Not Dead and Gone. They write their own music, and it's good. This past Saturday, I saw these guys rip out at The Cathedral. They played a tight set that consisted of eight songs, all from their demo "No Unsolution."

Spiro coughs.

SPIRO

"Milky, you're a fantastic soloist."

Milky burps.

MILKY

"Thanks. And by the way, we're a speed metal band, not a metal band."

SPIRO

"Yes. Speed metal, sorry. So how long have you been playing?"

MILKY

"No one knows."

SPIRO

"Can I ask who your influences are?"

MILKY

"You just did."

SPIRO

"So, who are your gods?"

MILKY

"What are you talking about?"

SPIRO

"Let's move on. Tell me, what do you think of the local music scene?"

MILKY

"Good question; I will tell you. It stinks."

SPIRO

"Anything else you'd like to say?"

MILKY

"Are you going to air this?"

SPIRO

"Yes."

SOUND BITE: Dead and Gone will be performing at the V.F.W. in Burghville on April 22.

The interview was horrible, but Dead and Gone had a decent crowd at the V.F.W. In fact, they had made enough money to professionally press their first demo. However, they did owe the Vets $150 for broken chairs and a damaged six foot by eight-foot folding table, which also happened to delay the Vet's "Sunday Pancake Posse Day."

Milky jumped off the pallet. "What kind of sick hippo would name their band Cry Baby?"

I gulped the rest of my orange soda and threw the empty can into the garbage and said: "My ode to redemption."

"You trying to be abstract?" he asked.

"Shea said to turn down the box."

"Fuck Shea!" He then laughed. "Imagine being named after a shitty baseball stadium."

"Meet the Mets, baby!" I shouted.

Milky was pumping a new band he discovered called "Crumbsuckers." The Crumbsuckers played a new style of music called "crossover," which fused the styles of speed metal and hardcore.

Milky turned down the radio. "Where's Handsome? Jerking off?"

"He's with Russo and Stacey at The Plaza."

"What's the word for tonight?"

"Grab a case," I said.

"What you fancy, Jimmy?" Milky asked with a very bad impersonation of a British accent.

"Coors Light sounds tight."

"What time are you heading out on Monday?"

"My flight is at seven."

"In the morning?"

"Nighttime, sweetheart."

"You're going to get to California around two in the morning," Milky said with concern.

"I go back in time, just like Captain Kirk."

Arty, a man with black-greasy hair who smelled like rotten beer, pushed his squeaky cart of empties to the counter. The 1990 heat had taken its toll on poor Arty. His bony arms were as tan as homemade brownies; his thin glasses were muggy and crooked. He wore a very old pair of Levi's, probably vintage style and worth some bucks. His baby-blue T-shirt was tight on his skinny chest. The head of his Marlboros pack peeped out of his sweaty shirt pocket. His old running shoes were held together by blue electrical tape.

Milky hit a button on the CD player as the music stopped. He then took the CD out of the player. "Speaking of California, have you ever heard of Jane's Addiction?"

"Who's Jane?" I asked.

"Jane is a band, my friend."

Milky held up a silver CD and smiled, dental fillings and all. "This, my friend, is probably one of the best CDs I have ever heard." He fed the player the CD and hit play. I was surprised to hear the beautiful voice of a woman speaking in Spanish.

"What is this?" I asked.

"Just listen."

After the woman finished speaking, the intro of the song began, which was fast and funky. After two measures, the rest of the band broke in. The sound was raw and dirty with a hybrid of metal and classic rock. The drummer played choppy, with a lot of drum rolls. The singer had a strange sounding voice. Everything about them resonated with me. There was something indeed special about their sound. "How did you discover them?"

"I read about them in some shit rock magazine and thought they seemed cool."

"They're fantastic!"

"I know! And the guitar player is intense."

Milky turned up the volume on the radio and put on a pair of yellow rubber gloves, as if he were about to perform a surgery. He grabbed a few cans and grimaced. "Jesus, Artie. Something die in your cart?"

"How you keep count with that shitty music?" Arty always spoke with missing verbs.

"Who says I'm counting."

Arty had been coming to Jack's Stack redemption since I started working there. And even before my working days at the Stack, I had seen him pushing his cart of empties around town. I sometimes referred to Arty as a "satellite bum," a bum that keeps circling around and around the city. Arty's world was a mystery to me. Maybe he was a victim of his own name—a starving ARTIST? Who would be the next ARTY? There was a rule at Jack's Stack. The rule stated that all empties be cleaned before being redeemed. We let Arty slip by.

And for the moment, it seemed as if life let Arty slip by.

Chapter 4

...and I'll probably be dead by then

After Mr. Shea handed me a check for $119.56, I took a quick drive around town—my sort of last adieu to Burghville.

I drove along Riverbank Street, located on the outskirts of the city. Riverbank ran parallel with the Hudson River and the train line.

There was about a mile where the street began on a hill and then dipped toward the river and then back up again. At this section a train trestle built of stones ran parallel with the street.

Two entry ways went directly under the trestle and led to the waterfront called "Burghville Landing." I made a left turn at the first entrance and drove the Sentra into the parking lot. I killed the engine. As I stepped out of the car, the skin on my back peeled off the vinyl seat, as if I was stuck on fly paper. I grabbed my old 8mm camera out of the back seat.

Besides a bunch of dirty seagulls looking for scraps of food, I was the only one around. Sizing up the landing, it was hard to believe Burghville was once a thriving city.

A long time ago, the waterfront was a hustling and bustling place. People came down to the river to shop, get a bite to eat, take the ferry across the Hudson to the city of Fordingtonville. Businesses like the shipping yards and the metal factories were booming in the early 1900's.

Now, with the birth of malls and plazas, all the factories and stores had been closed and condemned.

The day after the Burghville-Fordingtonville Bridge opened, the ferry closed.

Then there was urban renewal in the late sixties. Some blamed it for bringing crime and poverty to certain areas of downtown Burghville.

In 1952, some prestigious magazine named Burghville the "All American City." Now, in the heat wave of 1990, the city was plagued with drugs and crime, creating conditions of depression and despair.

I walked to the very end of the great wooden pier that extended above the water. I lit a cigarette. I turned on the camera as a breeze came off the river.

Looking through the camera lens, I could see in the distance cars and trucks driving along the two Burghville- Fordingtonville bridges. Near the concrete piers that held up the bridges were a bunch of sailboats. Looming in the background were the mountains.

I panned the camera up, ending on a couple of radio towers at the highest point of the mountain. Running through the center of the mountain, like a big zipper, was a gondola lift—now abandoned.

I moved the camera down from the mountain and ended on Bannerman's Island, known for Frank Bannerman's now deserted castle.

Panning the camera left, as far as I could turn, I ended on one of the narrowest sections of the Hudson River, sandwiched between Fordingtonville and Storm King Mountain. It was West Point. I thought about a paper I wrote in the sixth grade called "Washington's Link to Independence." It was about the building of the great chain that was laid across the Hudson River to stop the British fleet during the Revolutionary War. Batteries were placed along the forts to sink any British ship caught in the chain's web. But it was unknown if the chain could really stop the British. The chain was never tested because the British never came up that far up the river. Pieces of the chain reside in a historical site at West Point called "Trophy Point." On a very cold winter day, when I was seven, my father took me, my older brother and older sister to visit the chain and other tools of war at Trophy Point. I remember standing by the rock wall, looking at the river's narrow width and how the blue color twisted along the slope of the mountains. It was hard to digest that at one time there was war in the Hudson Valley.

I turned around and filmed the top of Washington's Headquarters, located in downtown Burghville. It was the Hudson Valley, this piece of land, where Washington would spill blood for America's independence. It was in the Hudson Valley that Washington denounced being King. And here I stood at the landing, surrounded by the spectres of early America, wondering if Burghville would someday become the special city it once was.

I turned off the camera.

Those who have read *On the Road* by Jack Kerouac know that Jack (very early in the book) got lost when he began his trip across the country. The place he ended up in was the Hudson Valley. I remember reading *On the Road* and wishing Kerouac had written more about the Valley. But Jack was on the move, and he had to get on with his journey.

Someone once told me things would have to get worse before a positive transformation could happen in Burghville. My response was: "I'll probably be dead by then."

Chapter 5

....as loud as The Who

After returning the car to my mother, I headed out to the Plaza by way of foot—just like old times.

It was close to nine o'clock. Above the horizon line, the sky looked like cotton candy as the sun had finished its game, but the humidity was going into extra innings, lingering for a stifling night. Walking along The Tundra, I saw a dead mouse near a storm drain. I stopped and stared at the small critter, wondering what led to its disaster. I wanted to kick it down the drain, but then decided to let nature take its course.

As I reached the corner of A/C's hardware, a parked pick-up truck and two human figures silhouetted were under the water tower.

I whistled.

One of the figures shot me the middle finger—it had to be Milky and Russo.

As I headed up to them, I could hear Megadeth blaring from Milky's blue pickup truck, mixing with the jazz of

Interstate 84. Milky bought the small truck for one grand. He convinced his parents to purchase it for him as an early graduation present. It was a lot of money for his working-class parents. Nevertheless, Milky had coerced them into considering the truck as an investment in his future. He was referring to his band, Dead and Gone. His parents took the bait, and Dead and Gone would no longer have to ask Russo's little grandmother (who liked to yell at him in Italian) if they could borrow her station wagon. Call it bad luck or maybe a warning but the first night driving the truck Milky ran over a skunk. A month later, on his way to a Dead and Gone show, he blew the radiator. But the cassette/radio player never let him down.

Walking along, I noticed Handsome was nowhere in sight. Reaching the top, I gave Russo and Milky the respectful handshake. I then bent over to catch my breath. Milky put his hand on my back and said, "My brother, you might need to quit the sticks."

I looked at Russo and responded: "How the hell do you smoke and play drums?"

Russo moved closer to me and said, "You sure you wanna know?"

"Tell me in another lifetime." I sat on the pavement and looked at the early quarter moon looming in the sky. The moon was tilted toward the earth and looked like a menacing eye upon the strange planet us humans inhibited. Below the banana shape, swarms of mosquitoes circled the light posts in The Tundra. And the letter "A" in the red A/C hardware neon light flickered for dear life; it looked like science fiction to me. So, like the dead mouse by the storm drain, I laid out on the pavement as I caught my breath. Reaching into my shorts, I grabbed my pack of smokes which contained one lonely cigarette. "Where's Handsome?" I asked.

"Last time I saw him, he took off with buzzhead," Russo said.

"I tell ya, those nuns fucked with his head," Milky said solemnly.

I thought it was odd that Handsome was with Stacey. She was tight about who she invited to her house. Her step-father was an intense man, and did not like her hanging out with boys in his house.

I lit my cigarette, took a drag and exhaled the smoke into the balmy air. "Can it get any hotter?" I said.

"Where you're going on Monday, you better get used to it," Milky said.

"It's a dry heat," I said and took another drag of my cigarette. I looked up at the barrel of the water tower to see the two flashing red beacon lights along the outer rim. "You know, if the water tower collapsed, it would roll down The Tundra and crush The Plaza."

"My dad says the State should knock The Plaza down and build a rest stop for the Interstate," Russo said.

"I like The Plaza just the way it is," Milky said.

Russo took a few steps away from the truck. He looked up at the sky and said, "You know, Jimmy, when you get that fancy film degree, you should shoot our first video."

At the same time, Milky and I both looked at each other and rolled our eyes.

"We'll shoot it in the parking lot," Russo said.

"What parking lot?" Milky asked.

"This one... right here... at The Plaza. Make it real, you know? I can set up my drums right under the water tower. We can even tag 'Dead and Gone' on the tower. It would be to pay homage to those kids who got trapped up there back in '76."

"I think one of those kids was high," Milky added.

"I think one of them is now a lawyer," I said.

"Whatever. The point is that they made a mark. They became legends," Russo said. He then ran over to one of the tower's metal legs. He unzipped his shorts and began to pee on it.

"What did you get from the stack?" I asked Milky.

"It's a big surprise."

I heard Milky's hand rummaging through the ice-filled cooler in the flatbed of his truck. He pulled out a green can of beer on top of my chest and placed it next to me. "Cheers!" he shouted.

It was the green monster, Genesee Cream Ale, staring me in the face. "My last weekend hanging out and you steal a case of Genny?" I said heatedly.

"Fucking Shea was hanging around me like a buzzard," Milky said defensively.

"Better than nothing." I cracked open the green monster. "Cheers!" I then took a big gulp.

"Tell me, Jimmy," Milky asked curiously.

Oh no! I thought. By that first line of speech indicated Russo and Milky had been arguing about something before I had arrived. I don't think there had ever been a day that Russo and Milky did not dispute about something, and it was usually music related.

"What's the best Maiden song ever?"

"Killers," I said with no hesitation.

Milky shouted to Russo, "Ha! Told you!"

"What are you talking about?"

"Maiden."

He flapped his hand. "Forget that first singer, Paul Di'Anno shit. Dickinson made that band," Russo said while walking back to us.

"*Number of the Beast* was written for Di'Anno," Milky said.

"They wrote that album after Di'Anno left the band," I said.

"See. Told you," Russo said.

As Milky and Russo argued, I took another gulp of the green monster. Suddenly, there was a loud thrusting sound heard in the distance.

"Sounds like a C-5," I said, interrupting their debate.

"I heard you could fit two rigs in one of them," Russo replied.

The C-5 Galaxy was the largest military plane ever built. The C-5 was first introduced by the military in 1969. Its main function was for strategic airlift. There were only a few Air Force Bases that housed them. One of them was Stewart Airport, located a few miles from The Plaza. The Air Force had been conducting C-5 trainings for years at Stewart's. I would be departing from the same airport Monday evening.

There was another thrusting sound, as if the plane was lifting off.

"I heard The Who were as loud as the roar of a jet engine," Milky said.

Russo tried following up on Milky's nugget of knowledge, but his statement fell on deaf ears; the monster was now flying over the water tower. Just like Pete Townshend, the great guitarist of The Who, we couldn't hear a thing. In the night sky, the C-5 looked more like a black creature, with its red blinking lights on the giant wings. But I knew its color was camouflage. It seemed strange that the Air Force would paint the largest plane in the world camouflage.

But it was not the odd choice of color or the girth of the plane that was intriguing; it was the wake turbulence that fascinated me. I once saw a documentary about this subject. The airplane's wings leave a trail of vortex or small tornadoes when flying through the air; the bigger the plane, the bigger the trail. After a C-5 or a jumbo jet departs into the sky, the next plane departing would have to wait at least two to five minutes. The vortex from the previous aircraft could cause the ascending plane to lose control.

As the C-5 ascended into the night sky, the sound of cars and trucks along 84 returned. Our dazzled eyes moved away from the night sky and back to planet earth. And it was at that shocking moment when we were greeted by a shaved-headed Handsome.

"What have you gone and done!" Milky shouted.

Russo blanketed his face with his hands for a moment. He let down his hands and said, "Such an idiot."

Some things are better left unsaid, I thought. But one thing was paramount: Stacey had Handsome under her spell.

Milky grabbed a green monster and threw it at Handsome.

"You guys are a bunch of assholes!" Handsome shouted as the can exploded near his feet like a water balloon.

In an act of rebuttal, Handsome grabbed the foaming can, which was about to roll down The Tundra, and threw it back at Milky, missing him by afar.

"You look like a squirrel or something," said Russo.

"He looks like Sinead O'Connor in that weird video."

We all laughed.

I then said, "I kind of like that video."

"You're insane, Bailey," Russo said.

"Fuck you all," Handsome said. "This is the new look, and soon everyone will be rocking this style."

"Not this hairy Italian," Russo said, pointing to himself.

"Rocking this style?" Milky said. "What are you? Run-DMC?"

"You wait and see," Handsome said.

It was his go to motto: *Wait and see.*

Handsome looked at me. "Bailey knows what time it is. Right, Bailey? You know what I'm talking about?"

"Sure," I said while taking another gulp of the green monster.

And for the finale, he said, "I'm through with metal."

Russo smacked Handsome on the head. "Don't be a fucking ass with that chit chat."

Handsome reached for a green monster from the cooler.

"How did you get here?" Milky asked him.

"The bus."

"Stacey didn't come with you?" Russo smugly asked.

"She went to F.U.'s band practice. She said she's gonna stop by." He took a sip of the green monster, swallowed, and grimaced. "God this taste terrible." He took another sip, then said, "Stacey played me one of F.U.'s tapes. It's pretty good."

"They fucking suck," Milky said.

"You say that about every local band," Handsom said. "In fact, I don't think you ever heard them."

"They fucking suck," Milky said.

I crushed my empty pack of cigarettes and threw it on the pavement. I stood up and wiped off the pebbles that had caked onto the back of my legs. "I'm heading to the big W to buy some smokes." I hated asking for change, but I did not want to sit around and hear Handsome's chit-chat about F.U. and his pathetic new look.

"Hold on, Bailey," Handsome said.

At that moment, under the menacing moon, I knew Handsome had some issues on his mind.

He jogged up to me. "I think Stacey likes me." He took another gulp of the green monster.

"She's got a boyfriend. You heard his band today, remember?"

Handsome tossed the can, burped and replied, "I think she's through with him."

I was drawn to the flickering letter "A" as we got close to A/C's hardware store. I had never noticed before, but some birds built a nest in the hole of the letter A. Maybe one of the birds will get the dead mouse by the storm drain. I heard Handsome's voice fade back into my existence.

"....I left with her this afternoon on the bus. We went to her house... her parents were not home... I mean, we didn't do anything, you know, I mean... it was just cool hanging out. She has this really cool room, with all these neat posters. You ever hear of Sick of it All? They're huge in the scene."

"I think I heard of them," I said. "They're like a heavy punk band, right?"

"No, no, no... they're nothing like punk. Hardcore and punk are two totally different scenes, man. Punk is dead, anyway. Hardcore is the shit, now."

I didn't care.

We walked down the long concrete walkway toward the big W. The Plaza was quiet as Handsome continued with his comments about Stacey and the state of music. "Metal is all about commercialization. Hardcore is about awareness. Take Russo, he's always talking about drum technique and how great this drummer is and blah, blah, blah. And Milky is all about guitar licks. Hardcore ain't about that shit. The scene could care less about technique—it's all futile."

There was something off-beat about Handsome saying the word "futile."

He continued. "Stacey schooled me about all this. Hardcore is totally different than metal." He rubbed his bald head. "And that's what having a shaved head means, it means I don't conform."

We reached the big W and entered the store. The air conditioning felt fantastic. As we stood in line at the checkout, I reached into the pocket of my shorts and grabbed two sweaty dollar bills. There was an old lady ahead of us. She had a basket full of lime colored yarn and one of those freaking house and gardening magazines. I wanted to ask her what gardening could be done in Burghville during the summer of 1990—the lousy heat killed everything!

Handsome said, "There's also these kids in the scene called 'straight edge'. I guess they oppose drugs, they don't eat meat, or some shit like that. Supposedly they'll like fuck you up if they see someone drinking beer at a show—strange paradox, huh?"

He then ran down the candy aisle, grabbed a couple of cherry lollipops and quickly ran back to stand in line. "I really think Stacey likes me. Didn't you see her sitting on my lap this afternoon?" He looked around and quietly said, "Man, I was so hard."

The old woman paid the clerk and left with her goodies. I handed the clerk two dollars. "Eight quarters."

The woman working the register handed me the coins. "Thanks," I said.

Handsome placed the lollipops on the counter. The women kept glancing at Handsome's head, as if he were a piece of work at a modern art exhibit. Handsome paid her in nickels and lint. We then entered the vestibule. I fed quarters to the old machine in exchange for a shorter life. Handsome sucked his lollipop, looking like a low-budget version of Kojak.

"I know that Stacey is still dating that guy from F.U., but I think she's going to break up with him. You know what I mean?" he said while raising his eyebrows with a ho hum.

I pulled the lever below the Marlboro Lights logo. I grabbed the cigarettes and left the matches in the slot. I packed the cigarettes on my palm. Handsome grabbed the matches and stuck them in the pocket of his shorts.

Back out on the walkway, Handsome said, "I don't wanna get my ass kicked by the guy in F.U., so I'm gonna keep cool for a while. But I really think she digs me."

I lit a cigarette.

"Can I bum a smoke?"

I handed him one.

"You ready for the big trip on Monday?"

"Yeah, I guess. What are you gonna do this fall?" I asked.

"I don't know. Go to community college or something. But you know me, I wanna start a band."

"Sounds cool."

"Yeah, just gotta meet the right people. But I also have to get my driver's license."

I had no response.

"You think I should've shaved my head?" he asked seriously.

I shrugged.

"Come on, Bailey. You're always straight with me. You're not like Russo and Milky. You speak the truth." We turned the corner at A/C's.

"Truth?"

"Am I crazy for doing this?" he said pointing at his head.

"You know what I think about all this hardcore, metal, shaved head stuff?" I flicked my cigarette into the storm drain, right next to the dead mouse. "I think–"

Handsome interrupted me and said, "If I tell you something, you promise not to tell Milky or Russo?"

"Okay."

"She went down on me this afternoon." He gestured to his cock, as if I didn't know what he meant.

It was hard to believe he would lie about something like this. If he was lying, he would have first told Milky and Russo. Handsome has always been straight with me. I was the friend he could talk serious with, even though I did not want to listen. I knew Stacey better than any one of the guys. Why she would go down on him was beyond my grasp. This was bad news. But there was nothing I could do. I had a plane to catch in a few days. My answer was, "I won't say a word to the guys."

As we headed to the water tower, a can of beer exploded near us, followed by a chorus of laughter. Within the chorus, I heard a girl's voice. It was Stacey. She was sitting in the back of Milky's truck, holding a can of the green monster. Handsome grabbed the beer from the ground and took a swig as we walked toward the tower.

Handsome grimaced as he swallowed the beer. "Fuck! This is warm!"

"Poser!" Milky shouted back.

"Takes one to know one!" Handsome said.

"Oh! You're so original and witty," Milky replied.

I sat in the same location, with the pebbles caking onto the back of my legs.

Milky grabbed the old rusty A&P shopping cart near the water tower and dragged it along the old pavement. He flipped it upside down and sat on its brown and silver metal bars. "Stacey's got some big news she wants to share," he said. "But she wanted to wait for her boyfriend to get back." Russo rubbed Handsome's head. I couldn't see Handsome's face, but I knew it was as red as the A/C sign.

"Fuck you, Tony," Stacey said.

"Don't call me, Tony," Russo said sharply.

And that is truly the fact, Jack for Russo. Don't call him Tony.

"Give us the news," Milky said to Stacey.

"You'll never guess what happened," she said excitedly.

We all waited for it.

"F.U. got a show at CBGB!" she shouted.

"What the fuck is a CBGB?" Russo asked.

"It's a famous club in New York City. Bands like The Ramones and The Police played there before they were famous," I said.

Milky and Russo clapped their hands and whistled.

"You don't need to go to college, Bailey. You're too smart," Russo said.

"Really? You guys didn't know that?" I said.

"Are you metal geeks gonna listen to me?" Stacey barked.

"Go ahead, go ahead," Milky said.

"Guess who they're opening up for?"

"We've come this far," Russo said.

"Stomach Virus. Tomorrow night. Isn't that cool?"

"There is a band called Stomach Virus?" Milky asked.

"Yeah, they're huge in the scene and F.U. is opening up for them," she said.

"Hell yeah!" Handsome exclaimed.

"They have been trying to gig at CB's for a long time. What better luck than opening for Stomach Virus. And here's the best part. You all are going to come with me to the show."

Except for Handsome, we were all nonplussed.

"And you're going to learn something about hardcore, and maybe something about culture."

"I'm not going to the city for that bullshit," Russo said.

"Why not?" Handsome asked.

"I don't give a rat's ass about Stomach Virus. I could care less about F.U. and their low-tech music. And, most of all, I hate hardcore."

"Come on. It will be so much fun. All of us hanging out in the city. Think of all the excitement. The food. The culture," she said, as if she were selling real estate.

"What do you think about this, Milky?" Russo snorted and laughed and then added: "Are you down for some culture?"

"What about Jimmy?" Stacey asked.

"What about me?"

"It'll be a big bang for your last weekend," she said.

It was a lie. I knew she wanted us to go to the city, because she could not go anywhere without a crowd. I'd bet my airfare to college that F.U. did not invite her to the show, posing the question if she was still dating the lead singer.

"If Bailey goes, then I'll go," Russo said.

"What do you think, Bailey? Ready for some goddamn culture in the city?" Milky asked.

They all looked at me, waiting.

I knew Stacey was up to something.

Even when I saw her earlier that afternoon, with her red lipstick and fishnets, there was a strange vibe emitting from her, as if she was hiding something.

I wanted to know what her real motivation was for inviting us. Plus, I had nothing better to do. I looked at the flashing letter "A" on the A/C sign, and replied, "Sure, I'll go."

Suddenly, I heard a loud sounding car. The noise was familiar.

We all looked toward The Tundra and saw a black Trans-Am creeping along.

It was James LeBleau. It had been a long time since I had seen him.

"Now there's someone who doesn't forget his roots," Russo said.

No one could argue with that. LeBleau did not camouflage his true colors.

I watched the Trans Am's cherry brake lights brighten as it reached the mouth of The Tundra.

And within a few seconds, he drove onto Route 32. No tires screeching, nothing dramatic.

He just drove off.

Chapter 6

Eleven, Eleven

Milky's truck rumbled like an old boiler as we waited for the traffic light to turn green. Russo and I drew the shortest straw and had to ride in the truck's flatbed. We were lucky the duration to the train station was only ten minutes. The lousy part was Russo and I had to lie on our backs in case we passed any State Troopers.

The truck's engine revved as we slowly moved under the light.

Handsome, who had the pleasure of sitting between Milky and Stacey, popped his shaved head out of the little rear window, as if he were a bird vacating in a hole of an oak tree. He shouted: "Don't forget to cover yourselves when we reach the toll booth!"

Russo, chewing gum, yelled back. "No shit, you skinny idiot!"

"This is my last weekend. How did I get the back of the truck?" I said to Russo.

Russo blew a bubble with his gum. After it popped, he said: "Life is a bitch, my friend." He then pulled out the pink wad of gum from his mouth and jammed it on the side panel as the truck began to accelerate.

Milky shifted gears as the truck picked up speed. We were heading 84 west bound and would soon cross the Burghville-Fordingtonville Bridge.

Russo and I bounced a bit until we were at a set cruise. The vibration from the muffler tingled like an electric shaver. Russo's sweaty arm kept bumping into me. It was bad enough his white T-shirt, which had spots of sweat that looked like a Rorschach blot, exposed his black and hairy armpits. Indeed, Russo was hairy—hairy enough to scare the sharpest razor. Case in point: he once told me that he began shaving in the eighth grade.

As I stared up at the cream-colored sky, I heard the squall of the truck's tires riding over the pavement suddenly turn smooth and harmonious. And within seconds, I was looking straight up at the rusty beams of the bridge that arched over the Interstate. Watching the beams climb higher and higher into the hazy sky, I knew we were crossing the middle point. Shortly after the arches faded, we headed toward the tolls. Milky down shifted as the truck jerked, causing Russo's sticky arm to bump into me again.

I shouted, "We're off the bridge!"

I reached for the baby-blue wool blanket Russo used to set his drums on top of. It was covered with drum stick shreds, due to his abusive drum playing. At one gig, at a bowling alley in Poughkeepsie, I saw him hit a cymbal so hard, he broke the cymbal stand in half.

I covered both of us with the wool blanket. And for a few minutes, that seemed like ions, we stopped and crawled to the tollbooth.

"It's like being nailed to the cross," Russo shouted.

"Thank god it's not rush hour," I said.

The humidity was never fun, especially under a smelly-wool blanket full of small wood ships and a hairy sweat hog; it was like hair sticking to a half-eaten lollipop. And it was in a situation like this that Russo (just to be an asshole) would have farted. Lucky for me he didn't.

Milky shifted gears as we picked up speed. We lifted the blanket and threw it into the corner of the flatbed. I took a deep breath as a sudden gust of sticky air strangely cooled me.

Milky pulled into the parking lot of the train station and found a spot near the boarding platform. I was surprised to see more pavement than vehicles. Then I remembered it was Saturday. If it was a weekday, the commuters would have filled the lot.

Milky killed the engine. I wiped the drum shreds off my sweaty T-shirt.

"I better get a window seat on the train for this," Russo said.

"There's nothing but window seats on the train," Stacey said.

All five of us headed to the small tunnel that led under the boarding platform.

"It just dawned on me. I don't think I've ever seen you wear a pair of shorts. Why is that?" Russo asked Milky.

"It could be that I'm not a sweat bag like you," Milky replied.

"Don't shit in your pants, man. I'm just making an observation."

Because I had been friends with Milky since kindergarten, I was the only one out of the bunch who knew why he didn't wear shorts.

The tragedy (not accident) had occurred on a March afternoon in the winter of 1985. School was closed due to a storm that delivered thirteen inches of packed snow. On snow days and weekends the neighborhood kids headed to Powder Hill at Powell Country Club to sleigh ride. Powell Country Club was a private golf course, and for some strange reason they let the public sleigh ride on the course's hills.

Powder Hill was located on the fourteenth (par five) fairway; it was the steepest incline on the course and ran parallel with a line of oak trees. On that day, Milky was the only kid who brought a toboggan sled.

Milky's family was always buying eccentric or unpopular things. When everyone was buying a VCR, his family had purchased a Betamax—which happened to have better resolution than a VCR.

Probably the most unusual item was the Magnavox Odyssey2 video game console. In the early 1980s, everyone had the Atari 2600, Intellivision or Colecovision. But not Milky. His parents had bought him the Odyssey2, what Milky called the PBS version of the video console games. It even had a keyboard to be used with their educational games. Strangely, the games of the Odyssey2 were modeled after well-known games of the early 1980s. But they weren't the real ones. I often thought it was these types of purchases that shaped Milky's desire to take chances on things that most people needed group approval. Not sure if that made sense, but that's what I felt.

So the toboggan sled fit in well with the aforementioned oddities. It was a Christmas present given to Milky by his grandfather. Because the toboggan had a flat bottom and was made of thin wood, it was much faster than the average cheap plastic sled.

Not knowing the science of a toboggan sled or kinetic energy for that matter, Milky and his two cousins fitted themselves onto the candy cane shaped sled like packed sardines.

With a couple of pushes, the three plowed down the fairway. No one worried about the thirty yards of flat fairway past the hill; no one shrugged that the stretch of land led to a manmade pond (except for lousy golfers), and nobody flinched that the pond was half frozen due to a warm winter. That was because no one in the neighborhood, except for Milky, owned a lousy toboggan sled.

Throughout the day the sun caused the snow to turn wet and packed, making the sled move faster. The toboggan suddenly turned into a panic sled as Milky and his friends plowed toward the half-frozen pond.

Milky's cousins abandoned ship, leaving him to fend for himself.

Now alone, he piloted the sled away from the pond and toward the oak trees. He then leaned to his right, while sticking his left knee into the snow as a brake.

The toboggan barely passed between the oaks. But Milky's leg nicked the bark of the tree, as the jagged edge tore into his jeans, slicing his skin like pulled pork.

Ten feet later, the toboggan came to a stop on the par four, fifteenth fairway.

Milky rolled off the sled as blood from his leg seeped into the snow like spilled red wine on a white rug.

Within an hour, Milky had arrived at the hospital, and by then end of the snow day he came home with twenty-one stitches on his leg.

It was possible that Powell Country Club was liable for the accident. But Milky's parents were not friends of revenge. They were glad that their only son did not lose a leg. That next evening, Milky's dad chopped the toboggan into pieces with an ax, and he used it for that evening's fire. I never understood why Milky thought his scar would be so frightening to the eyes. Maybe it was some ego thing? Was the scar a perpetual reminder of his failure to control and guide the toboggan through the tree line? Sure, Milky had lots of talent. Yet he surely had no talent to live with failure.

Now, drifting my attention away from Milky's mystery scar, I noticed Stacey was wearing those sexy fishnets under her shorts again. Her eyelids were painted with black eyeliner, and her lipstick was blood red. She also wore the white colored F.U. shirt again. Handsome fashioned a pair of green khaki shorts, which exposed his hairless legs. He had on a new black Sick of it All T-shirt, and every other minute he rubbed his shaved head like he was lost in a sunflower field.

As we walked through the moist and cool tunnel under the tracks, Russo asked me, "What do you think, Jimmy? Good place to piss?"

"Sure," I said.

While Russo marked his territory in the tunnel, the rest of us walked up the steps to the big platform. The Fordingtonville train station was nothing fancy. It was simply a long boarding platform with a few benches, and a large train timetable. I lit a cigarette and approached the timetable. "What time is the train, again?" I asked.

"For the hundredth time. Eleven! Eleven!" Stacey shouted.

I moved closer to the timetable and read some of the train stops along the Hudson: Cold Spring, Tarrytown, 125th Street and the last stop, good old Grand Central Terminal.

I looked across to the Hudson River at Burghville. The first visible landmarks were The United Methodist's church steeples that tickled the sky. West of the steeples were St. Patrick's two moldy-colored bell towers. Looking toward the shore of the river, I saw the train trestle near Burghville Landing.

Returning my eyes to the boarding platform, I spotted a suit and tie guy sitting on one of the benches, reading the *New York Times*. Somehow the man found a section on the bench that was not covered with white and brown seagull shit. I was baffled that he could be cool and confident in his black, sun absorbing suit, while reading the business section. There was not an ounce of sweat on him.

I lived in a commuter area and knew a number of people who took the train to the city for work. It seemed so awful to live life by the train. But what did I know, anyway? My only job experience was to sort and count the local drunks and one abstract-homeless man's empties.

Russo joined us on the platform. "This reminds me of a movie I once saw—had these real funny noises, and there were these three tough guys waiting at an empty train station..." Russo waited for someone to follow up. No one answered.

"Sergio Leone's *Once Upon a Time in The West*," I said.

Russo clapped. "You're a god, Bailey."

"And you're a psycho, Russo," Milky said.

"Did you know the studios wanted Henry Fonda to change the color of his eyes to brown?" I said.

"Really," Russo said.

"Yeah, but Leone said no because the audience knew Fonda's blue eyes, which would make his character even more menacing."

"That's fucking awesome," Russo said.

Stacey watched Russo band his hair into a ponytail. "You should let me shave that mop off of your head."

"Let me tell you a tale about my family. It's easy to comprehend. Everyone in my family is bald. So, I'm going to keep my hair the way it is, until it decides to fall the fuck off."

"You sure you know where we're going?" Milky asked Stacey.

"I always take the train with F.U.," she said.

"That can't be good, then," Milky said jokingly.

She pushed Milky and smiled. "You're just jealous because they got a show in the city, Robert!"

"I do not agree with that statement, but I do agree that F.U. suck balls," Milky said.

"Why didn't you go with F.U?" Russo asked Stacey.

I wanted to ask the same thing, but I knew Stacey better than anyone, and I did not need to venture into that territory.

"They had no room in the van for me," she said.

"That's because you have a fat ass!" Milky shouted.

"I do not!" she said as she bumped her ass into Milky's thigh.

I watched Handsome try to hide his jealousy as she flirted with Milky.

"What's up with you, Handsome?" Russo said. "You look like you're ready to drift off and die."

"Is it okay that I have nothing to say?"

Russo guffawed. "When have you ever had something to say?"

"Have you ever been to the city?" Milky asked Handsome.

"Here comes the train. And that son of a bitch better have air conditioning!" Russo shouted.

I looked to the north and saw the silver train approaching. I couldn't agree more. Air conditioning was a necessity.

The train's brakes squeaked as it slowly reached the platform. All of us gathered closely. I looked back to see the man sitting on the bench folding his paper—nothing new for him.

The doors opened as we boarded the silver tube.

The train was called *The Metro North*. The colors of the seats were wine red and navy blue. The windows were tinted like a limousine.

There were advertisements in every direction. One ad asked if you were happy with your car insurance; another one displayed the musical *Cats*. But the meanest ad was the one that said: NO SMOKING PERMITTED.

Fordingtonville was the second stop along the Hudson line, and there was hardly anyone aboard the train, and we took advantage of it.

Russo sat behind me and Milky sat across from Russo. Handsome sat next to Stacey.

I chose my seat next to the river, so I could see the sights.

The doors closed, and then the train jolted as we began to move. I looked through the tinted window as we picked up speed. Burghville was drifting away as we began our journey along the Hudson.

A few minutes into the ride, the door between the train carts opened as a gust of engine noise plowed in.

The conductor, who was dressed in all blue, walked toward us. He had a thick mustache, and he wore a funny hat that said METRO NORTH.

We all dug into our pockets to pay him. I handed the man a sweaty Andy.

The fare was $16.50 for a round-trip ticket.

The conductor did not look happy. He punched some holes into a small ticket and then clipped it onto my seat. He handed me my change and ticket stub.

My father told me to stick my money into my sock, to prevent thieves from pickpocketing me. Probably the safest way to hide my money was to eat it.

After the conductor finished with us, he headed off to the next cart like he was entering perdition.

I looked out my window and saw Bannerman's Island approaching. The castle looked as if it was about to fall into the river. I noticed someone had tagged in blue spray paint on the wall BLACK SABBATH RULES 71.

During the American Revolutionary war, Washington had used the island to store ammunition. Now, in 1990, the castle was an ad for a great metal band. Over the loudspeaker we heard in a strong city accent, "Next stop, Cold Spring Harbor."

Russo asked, "You guys see the preview for *GoodFellas*?"

"That's the new Scorsese movie with De Niro and Pesci coming out in a few weeks. Scorsese is a God!" I said.

"What the fuck is a Scorsese?" Russo asked.

"You sure you're Italian?" I asked.

"I've seen the *GoodFellas* trailer," Handsome said. "It looks good. Definitely want to see it."

"But is your mom going to let you see an 'R' rated movie, or is she coming with you as your date?" Russo said.

We all laughed.

"Good job up keeping up the clown antics," Handsome said.

"Drum roll, please," Russo chuckled.

Milky drummed on the seat.

"Your comebacks are lamer than a game of Pac-Man at Pizza Hut," Russo said.

"Pac-Man? That is SOOOOOOOOOOO nineteen-eighties," Stacey said.

"Do you guys know that Stacey used to have a poster of Tom Cruise from *Top Gun* in her bedroom?" Russo said.

She shot him a nonplussed look. "Go masturbate a potato, Anthony."

"You know what I can't wait for? The day they make a movie with De Niro and Pacino," said Russo.

"They did. It's called *The Godfather* part two," replied Handsome.

"I mean acting together in the same scene, you worthless ding dong."

"Who's a better actor? Pacino or De Niro?" Milky asked Russo.

"Don't even get on the Phil Donahue show with that shit," Russo said.

"*Taxi Driver* is the best De Niro movie," Stacey said.

"How about *The Deer Hunter*? De Niro was great in that one. Cimino is a God," I said.

"Who are these people you keep talking about?" Russo asked.

"Are you sure you're Italian?" I asked again.

"Bailey, you're not allowed to take part in this conversation. Deep thinker movie watchers are disqualified," Russo said.

"You still didn't answer my question," Milky said to Russo.

"What?"

"De Niro or Pacino?"

"It's like comparing apples to oranges," Russo said.

"Okay, so what do you like better, apples or oranges?" Milky asked.

My attention drifted away from Russo and Milky as I looked at the passing landscape. We were heading under the Bear Mountain Bridge, which connected Route 9 to Route 9W at the narrowest point of the river. Because the mountains were so close to each other, the glacier dug deeper into the riverbed, making this the deepest part of the Hudson River.

"You think Milky would kill me if I told Russo about his big scar on his leg?"

I turned to see Stacey, who was now sitting next to me.

"You promised me you would never tell anyone. It's a secret. Remember?" I said.

"What? That Milky crashed into a tree while sleigh riding with his goofball cousins? So stupid," she said.

"If you knew Milky like I do, it's kind of a big deal. Remember? It's a secret."

Stacey retrieved a pack of Starburst from her small purse. "It's a stupid secret." She handed me a lemon-flavored one. "I hate the yellow ones."

"Thanks," I said as I ate the yellow Starburst. "Bored with Handsome?"

"He went to find the bathroom."

"They have bathrooms on the train?" I don't even know why I asked that unimportant question.

"I guess," she said.

Behind me Russo and Milky were bickering about the De Niro movie, *Raging Bull* and the Pacino film, *Sea of Love.*

"You're lucky," she said.

"What did I win?"

Stacey jabbed me with her elbow. "No! You're getting out of Burghville."

"You could leave, too. Burghville is not a prison, you know."

She shrugged and said, "Yeah, maybe." She plopped another Starburst into her mouth, cherry flavored. "So, you're really going to study film in L.A.?"

"I don't want to be a shrink like my father."

She raised her hands like a fortune teller and said, "I'd always pictured you as a writer, or an English major, you know, something artsy-fartsy, not a Hollywood hotshot."

"Well, if I had a choice, I rather do nothing."

"And be like the rest of your friends?"

"What are you talking about?"

"You think Dead and Gone are really going to make it?" she said.

"They knocked down the Berlin wall, didn't they?"

"Metal is so boring. People want something new," she said.

"Didn't we already have this conversation?"

"You have quite the memory, James."

"There will always be an audience for metal," I said.

"Think about it, Jimmy. The odds are against them. In a few years, they'll all be married with kids. They'll have low paying jobs and probably be miserable with credit card debt."

"Milky with kids? Are you kidding me?" I said.

"Is there another Milky secret I should know about?" Stacey asked enticingly.

"Come on. If nothing happens. Well, at least they'll have their memories, at least they've tried," I said.

"That could be your first screenplay, Sir James."

Maybe she was right. I know Russo thought the band was going to be huge. What would happen if they were not? What was the backup plan? I couldn't see Russo in the cement business, like his dad and his brothers. But I know Milky could survive.

"You should be a record executive, you know, an A&R rep," I said, changing the topic.

"What's an A&R rep?"

"The people who go out and sign unknown bands."

I did not expect her to respond to my suggestion. I should have known better then to tell her what she could be good at.

"Are you excited to go to the city?" she asked.

"Sure."

"I can't wait. I LOVE the city!"

Handsome walking back to his seat. A big spot of water was on his shorts.

"Urine goes in the toilet bowl," Russo said.

"Hah! Hah! Fuck you, and *The King of Comedy* is De Niro's best movie."

"Hey, your boyfriend is back," I whispered to Stacey.

She looked at me for a long moment. "It's not what you think," she said sharply. She stood, walked up a couple of rows and sat by herself.

A few seats up, I could see Stacey's reflection in the window. She had her hand over her face.

Why should I care?

I looked back at the Hudson. Man, the white noise from the train's air conditioner was making me drowsy.

The Cathedral Theatre
Presents

Friday, April 6

DEAD AND GONE

With special
guest

Paine In The Neck

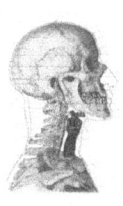

HUDSON VALLEY
METAL

Tickets $7

Doors Open at 8pm
22 First St, Poughkeepise, NY

CHAPTER 7

The Show

Stacey always got sad when she heard the song, "Born to Run" by Bruce Springsteen. It was her father's favorite song. And because Stacey's dad had died in a horrible motorcycle accident in May of 1987, the song had a lot of meaning for her. Her dad was forty-two years of age when he sank his 1972 Harley-Davidson Sportster and himself into Bear Creek.

The manner in which Stacey described her dad, surprisingly, did not fit the jeans, long hair and bearded biker type. In fact, he was a suit and tie guy.

Her dad was a successful real estate agent, a serious businessman. But his road to success was not a simple one.

When Stacey's dad was in his early twenties, he took part in the hippie movement of the late sixties. He went to Woodstock and smoked weed. He expressed his outrage about the Vietnam War. He liked The Rolling Stones. And he opposed corporate America.

To him, at that time, the values of the fifties had been raked and bagged away like a pile of orange leaves dancing in the eve of October.

But it wasn't long when those ideals and principles he vehemently followed in the sixties began to melt away.

It was 1970 when Stacey's dad had turned twenty-five. There were bills to pay; it was time to get a job—maybe even a career. And he could not keep his eyes off that sexy Italian girl who worked at the hamburger grill. It was probably those daunting green eyes that made him marry Stacey's mom.

Shortly after, in the winter of 1971, Stacey's mom had two small legs kicking in her belly.

Nine months later, Stacey Angela Polanski breathed air on planet earth.

Things were indeed changing for her dad. It was the seventies. The country was in a recession. Rock and roll had lost its steam, and disco was littering the sound waves. Salvation came in 1975, when this singer from New Jersey began making waves with a song called: "Born to Run," a song, lyrically, that seemed to capture the zeitgeist of the decade. It was at that same time when Stacey's dad had got a job as a loan researcher at a local bank. He worked his way up to being a loan manager. But in 1980, when working at the bank no longer satisfied him, he took a job at a real estate company.

Maybe it was seeing those happy couples getting their loans for a new home that interested him in the real estate world.

Or maybe it was the untapped upstate land that convinced him. It was the early eighties when the big malls began popping up in the Hudson Valley. More and more fast food restaurants and strip malls soon followed.

Burghville was shaping into a quintessential suburban town. And Stacey's dad was reaping the benefits of its metamorphosis. He was a hippie gone capitalistic.

Yet it was that day when he heard "Born to Run" on the radio that he longed for his youth, and those young and crazy ideals he once held—as cliché as it may sound.

Or maybe he was just having a midlife crisis?

Well, whatever it was, the song stuck to him like peanut butter in the mouth. With a nice chunk of money in the checking account, he bought himself a 1972 vintage Harley-Davidson Sportster.

The Sportster was the last of its kind to be completely built in Milwaukee, Wisconsin—if he knew it or not.

It was toward the end of March, when the air was fresh and the start of spring. It wasn't officially motorcycling season, but it was on a usually warm Saturday afternoon when Stacey's dad decided to go for a cool or an existential bike ride.

Halfway through the journey, he approached the sharp turn around Bear Creek Road and things were no longer good. The roads had not been clear of salt and debris from the winter season.

Stacey's dad hit a patch of salt around a sharp turn and....

Stacey had told me many things about her dad, and some of her father's stories I gathered from browsing the scrapbooks and photo album in her bedroom. She was a different person after he died. And I was intrigued by her persona. But I couldn't pinpoint exactly what it was that had attracted me to her.

I met Stacey at Dead and Gone's first headlining gig at The Cathedral in the spring of 1990.

I was up on the drum riser, tightening the lugs to Russo's left bass drum, while trying not to bump into the many microphones surrounding the chaotic drum set.

Dead and Gone had just finished their sound check, which I thought sounded fantastic. But Russo argued that the bass drums needed to be more "muffled," and asked if I could stick another pillow in each one of them.

I told him that I would be more than happy to stick one of them up his ass.

Russo was a bitch when it came to his drum sound, and I should know, for I signed on to be his drum tech. Russo owned a black drum set made by a company called Tama. The choice was simple: He bought a Tama set because Dave Lombardo of Slayer played them.

For some cosmic reason, when I grabbed the last lug from the drum bag, I felt someone was watching me. I slowly turned my head and saw this red-headed girl standing near the right-side PA speaker. She was looking up at me.

The club had not opened. But somehow, she got inside. Big Lou, the club owner, must have let her in, I thought.

The redhead fashioned a big leather jacket that hung half-way over her jean skirt. Her long black boots went up to her knees and the rest of her legs were bare to the lip of her skirt. She smoked a cigarette while sizing up the club.

And then the bouncer, a small and stocky fellow who looked to be in his forties, jumped onto the stage, destroying my trance. He was wearing a faded Rolling Stones shirt, which featured the band's classic picture of the big red lips.

"We're opening the doors," he snapped.

He pushed a button on the wall and down came the black curtain.

But just before the curtain kissed the stage floor, the red-head and I made eye contact.

Behind me a loud *boof, boof* made me jump.

"Sounds good, Jimmy!"

I frowned to see Russo laughing behind the drum set. His long hair was pulled back into a ponytail. He had a dash of black eyeliner and wore a black tee shirt and black jeans. Everything was black in the metal scene.

"You're an ass!" I said.

"Better than a dick."

"Please stop the bad banter," Milky said as he joined us. He was also wearing a black shirt.

"What's going on outside?" Russo asked.

"You should see all the people in the parking lot—it's going to be nuts tonight," Milky said.

"Last time we played, the only thing in the parking lot was bird shit."

"You always amaze me," I said to Russo.

Russo jumped off the drum riser. "Where's Handsome?"

"He went down to the pizza parlor with the rest of the band," Milky said.

"Let's get off the stage," I said.

"Good idea," the bouncer added.

"We're the headlining act, you know?" Milky said.

"It only gets worse from here," The bouncer said as he headed to the stage door.

"The Rolling Stones suck!" Russo shouted.

"No they don't," Milky said.

We proceeded to the door, which led us to a small and dimly lit room.

Most of the room was filled with "Reign of Terror's" instruments. They were the second band on the bill. Since the opening act's equipment was already set up on the stage, Reign of Terror had to keep their equipment in the little room. Second was a great slot, especially for an unknown band. For one, by the time the second band begins, most of the club is filled with people. And two, everyone is pretty comfortable and ready to rock.

However, being second, you had little time to set up your equipment. There were time constraints in between acts. Add in a feisty stage crew, there can be a greater chance for instruments to go awry and blood pressure to rise.

One time I forgot to fasten the wing nut to Russo's china cymbal. And during the second song, Russo (being a hard-hitting drummer) smashed the china, knocking it off the stand and sending it into orbit.

The cymbal bounced onto the stage with a wicked splash, and then did a nosedive, landing into the arms of a teen boy in front of the stage.

The kid bolted to the exit door with the cymbal.

Seeing his expensive cymbal run amuck, Russo jumped off his set, dove into the crowd, and dashed through the exit door.

Since this kid happened to be the only person wearing a Queensrÿche tee shirt, Russo was sure to capture him.

I and the rest of the band headed through the loading dock and out into the parking lot.

Russo had wrestled the kid to the ground. "Who do you think you are, stealing my shit?"

"I'm doing you a favor, man," the kid said.

"How so?"

"You overplay the china."

Russo unwrinkled his eyebrows and softly said, "Overplay?"

"You're showing off," the kid said as he unraveled himself.

They both got up and began to talk like gentlemen.

"What about that song we were just playing. You think I was playing too much double bass?"

The kid took a deep breath and said: "Ever since Dave Lombardo did that double bass solo in 'Angel of Death', everybody wants to play fast double bass. Nobody listens to the music anymore."

I thought the kid was throwing out generalizations.

But Russo and the kid, whose name was Jacob Winters, windup becoming good friends.

Jacob showed up at all the shows, always wearing a Queensrÿche T-shirt. And Russo became a better drummer after his encounter with him. Then one day, Jacob's father got laid off at IBM.

A month later, Jacob moved. And that was that.

But nothing was tougher than being the first act of the show.

Of course, the first act had the great pleasure of having their instruments already set up on stage. They also got a sound check before the club opened. However, because the first band had to set their instruments in front of the headlining act's equipment, they had little room to move on the stage. They also had to perform when the club was still letting in the crowd. And the crowd (if they're lucky to have one) is usually sheepish during the first few songs.

While playing thrash or speed metal—whatever you want to call it—you expect the crowd to mosh to your songs.

There seemed to be a ritual to moshing. At a certain part in a song or riff, the crowd would erupt into a frenzy. Moshing or slam dancing, depending on what scene you're from, was nothing more than a release. There was nothing deep about it. Fans feed off the energy from the band, and the band feeds off of the fan's energy.

And if the band was good, they would know how to control the energy, manipulate it—usually by the infamous mosh section in a song.

There was no better high than to see a crowd of kids go crazy for the music you have created, that's what Milky had told me.

Milky could write some incredible mosh parts. I mean, he knew what the audience wanted.

But for a new band, it's a different scenario.

I remember those early Dead and Gone shows when a hundred or so metal kids would stare at them, arms folded and all. And that was the toughest part about being a new band: no one knowing your music. That was another thing Milky had shared with me.

The house music turned on as we moved through the backroom.

I was taken aback to see John Volpe, the guitarist and singer for the band, Paine in the Neck.

He was leaning next to the pay phone, smoking a cigarette and looking fidgety.

Volpe had a dyed green mohawk and wore black eyeliner like a gazelle.

His parents owned one of the best diners in Burghville, plainly called VOLPE'S.

The Volpe's were good friends with Russo's family, and that is how Russo and John became friends.

Volpe's band used to be called "Pain the Neck." But he thought adding the "E" on to the end of the word "Pain" would give the name more depth as well as a sense of irony.

Paine in the Neck was the opening act, and it was their first big show.

Volpe's band was what I would call a joke band. No, they weren't terrible or a fiasco to the music community.

Rather, their songs were usually small jokes or funny anecdotes on daily life.

They were simply a tongue and cheek band. Or as Volpe had once said to me, "A tonguing the cheek band." I even think they had a song called, "Blueberry Yogurt Makes Me Vomit in B-Flat."

"Volpe, you look like you're ready to die. What's the matter?" Russo asked.

Volpe's hand shook as he took a drag of his cigarette. "I'll tell you what's the matter. They're gonna crucify us—just like Christ at the age of thirty-three."

"You begged me to put your band on the bill," Russo said.

"This is a fucking nightmare!" Volpe cried.

"Relax, man," Milky said.

"It's all about technique, they want technique," Volpe said. "Metalheads don't like bands like mine. They don't want three chord songs. We're a simple band with simple songs." Volpe turned to me. "You know what I'm talking about, right, Jimmy?"

"Sure," I said.

"You don't know if they're gonna hate you," Russo said, trying to comfort him.

"Easy for you to say. You guys got a popular demo with a cool logo and great production value."

While Volpe talked, I kept glancing at the writing on the walls of the back room. Most of the scribbles and big letters were messages left by the bands that had played The Cathedral. It was hard to imagine all of the famous musicians and bands that had hung out in the back room. With that in mind, it was quite strange to see Volpe suffer from stage fright.

Volpe dropped his cigarette and threw his hand over his mouth. "I think I'm gonna puke."

"Get'em to the bathroom," Milky commanded.

We helped Volpe through the backroom to another door that led to a set of stairs, which led to the hallway where the bathroom resided.

The bathroom, which respectively smelled like urine, had graffiti and band stickers plastered on all walls.

Russo helped Volpe into one of the stalls. And within a few moments, Volpe painted the bowl.

"Hey, Volpe. Looks like your dad made the goulash special tonight," Russo said.

We all laughed.

"You could make a new song out of this experience," Milky said.

"I think he already did," I added.

"Yeah! Goulash in B minor," Russo said.

"Very fucking funny!" Volpe said as he flushed the toilet. He then walked out of the stall and approached the mirror. He turned on the faucet and wiped the bits of his regurgitated dinner off of his face.

"How does one vomit with a mohawk?" Milky asked.

"You all right, man?" Russo asked.

"You guys aren't going to tell my band about this?"

"If they find out, we'll tell them you were pumped up on drugs—sounds better than stage fright," Russo said.

Milky was suddenly drawn to the wall. "Those fucking hair metal bastards." He spotted Cry Baby's flyer taped askew above one of the urinals. In one quick stroke, Milky ripped the flyer off the wall and stuck it onto Volpe's leather jacket.

Volpe screamed, "Now you fucking jinxed me, you fucking bear!"

We all ran out of the bathroom. Volpe bolted after Milky. "Get it off of me," he shouted.

I saw the redhead girl exiting the women's room.

On stage it was difficult to see her face, but in the ugly fluorescent lights, she was gorgeous.

Her hair was shiny and straight. She had green eyes that pulled you under like an undertow, and I was drowning.

"Hey, aren't you guys in Gone and Dead," she asked.

"You mean Dead and Gone," Russo said.

"Sure," she said.

"Yeah, me and that guy you just saw chasing the kid with the green hair." Russo put his hand on my back. "And this here is Jimmy the Great, our roadie."

The redhead shot me a half smile.

"What's your name?" Russo asked.

"Stacey."

"So I take it that you heard our demo, Stacey."

"Yeah, I heard it—it's all right and all. Don't get me wrong, your band is neat and all, but in all truths, what else is there to do in suburbia? Right?" Stacey turned to me, leaving Russo twisting and hanging like a piñata, and asked, "You got a light?"

"I'll be at the bar, talking to Big Lou," Russo said, and he walked off.

Stacey stuck a cigarette into her mouth as I lit the head. I lit one for myself as well. "I think you made him mad."

"I like Dead and Gone. I just don't like it when cocky musicians beg for compliments."

"I've never seen you around."

"I've never seen you either. Isn't life peculiar?"

"Indeed, it is."

"What's up with your friend with the green mohawk?"

"What do you mean?" I asked.

"I heard his middle name is Ralph."

I stared at her with confusion.

"You know," Stacey said as she stuck her finger into her mouth. "RAAAALPH."

I laughed nervously and said, "Those bathroom walls are pretty thin."

"And among other things," she added.

"That's Volpe. He's got stage fright."

"I like his hair," she said. "Different than all these metal clowns."

"You don't like metal, I take it?"

"Weird hanging in the hallway, don't you think?" she said, changing the topic.

"Let's head to the floor," I said.

The house music was loud as we walked through the club. There must have been over a hundred people already. It was hard to believe how fast Dead and Gone's popularity grew in the upstate scene. As we watched the fans enter the club, it seemed like every metal head looked the same: long hair, black metal shirts, and smoking the same brand of cigarettes. Man, all those warnings and all those health classes, and another generation gave in to tobacco. I was seventeen and my body could probably handle the nicotine for at least another ten years. Maybe? Possibly? I didn't want to think about my death. I lit another.

"Let's go to the bar and grab a table," I shouted over the music.

As we walked to the bar, I saw Milky and Russo talking to Big Lou, the owner of The Cathedral.

Big Lou was the fattest man I had ever seen. We usually found him sitting at the end of the bar, smoking cigarettes and reading the newspaper.

Sometimes Big Lou would fall asleep at the bar.

My brother, the expert in medicine, once told me it was because he was not getting enough air to his brain.

Although Big Lou did not take care of himself, he took special care of Dead and Gone. It was Big Lou who had given them their big break.

Stacey and I sat at a table near the bar.

"Why the short hair?" she asked.

"The simple answer is that my hair is too wavy, and looks like shit when it gets long."

"What's the abstract answer?"

I shrugged.

"Why the metal crowd and not the chess club or the literary club?" she asked.

"Why does the scene you hang out with have to define who you are?"

"Because it does. The fact that you hang with the metal scene pretty much makes you a metal head."

"I don't believe in labels," I said. "Call it what you will."

Stacey stared at me with a raised brow and smiled.

I tugged on her leather jacket. "Jacket is kind of big on you."

"It's my father's."

"Your dad a biker?"

"Stuffy in here," she said as she took off the jacket. She was wearing a Sex Pistols T-shirt.

"Big Lou doesn't turn the air conditioning on until the club is completely filled," I said.

"That doesn't seem practical."

"I know. But that's Big Lou for you."

A group of people crowded near our table.

Stacey grimaced. "Do you smell it?"

"What?"

She leaned close to me and then whispered into my ear. "Someone is wearing patchouli." I didn't know what she was talking about. But her mouth close to my ear had set me on fire.

"Hippie perfume."

She must have sensed my confusion.

"We can move somewhere else, if you want," I said.

"Do you want to go outside for a while?"

I knew if I left with her, I would miss the show. And Russo would bruise me up for leaving him with no drum roadie. Unlike the patchouli, her force was compelling.

We left the club and hung out in the parking lot. We heard the bands faintly as we sat on the hood of my car.

Judging by the claps and cheers, Paine in the Neck played well. It was an ironic moment for Volpe.

Not long after, me and Stacy drove off to some park and had sex. Then it ended.

The next day we would just be good old friends.

CHAPTER 8

Station of Stars and the 6 Train

It was quiet, and I felt like I was floating.

I slowly opened my eyes and saw my reflection in the train's window.

Beyond my reflection, I saw nothing but black.

I moved my head closer to the window, but my eyes couldn't fix on anything to tell if we were moving.

The last thing I remembered was the smooth walls of the Palisades along the Hudson.

The train's lights flickered as the air conditioning kicked back on. Everyone was asleep, except for Milky; he was reading the Arts and Leisure section of the *New York Times*—a sight to behold.

I stretched my arms, looked back through the window, and saw rail tracks in the far distance, as if we entered a tunnel.

The train's lights flickered again while the buzzing of the air conditioner went on and off.

I saw a burst of light through the window as we slowly pulled up along a boarding platform—kind of like the one in Fordingtonville. And then the train stopped.

Everyone awoke.

Milky folded the paper, stood and stretched. We joined in the afternoon stretch, adding yawns and bad breath to the air.

Over the loudspeaker, in a strong city accent, a voice said, "Welcome to Grand Central Station. Thank you for riding Metro North."

"About time," mumbled Russo with an unlit cigarette dancing on his lips.

We walked off the train and onto the boarding platform. It felt like we were in a gigantic basement. Our world of oak trees, furry mountains and a sultry sky were replaced with contorted pipes, cement, and a wretched stench of burning oil.

"This place smells like a boiler room," Russo announced.

"This way," Stacey commanded.

Putting our trust into Stacey as our guide, we melted in with the throng, walking in unison along the platform. It was stiff; I mean, no one said a word. Everyone just moved forward.

I had no idea where we were going.

At the end of the platform, I heard voices echoing.

The reverb of voices continued to grow as we walked closer and closer.

As we made a left turn, I saw nothing but gold. It was magnificent and immaculate.

Hundreds of people moved in all different directions in this cathedral of transportation.

Like the slotting of coins through a cigarette machine, they were coming in and out of portals to trains that could take you almost anywhere in the U.S.A. We were at the crossroads of mass transportation: Grand Central Terminal.

As we gravitated toward the information booth in the center of the station, I almost tripped over the shine from the floor.

Turning right, there were two sets of stairs that met, forming the shape of a U.

To the left, the flood of sunlight seeped through three gigantic arched windows above.

I looked up at the high curved ceiling and saw the mural of constellations.

The noise of the station drifted away as I eyed each one: Scorpio, The Big Dipper, and my favorite, Orion.

Most people were moving fast through the station, and it seemed as if they had no time for the beauty around them. I guess all things get boring, including the great things. For me, at least at that moment, Grand Central was the greatest place I had ever been. I wondered if the guys felt the same.

"I'm in the mood for a Yoo-hoo!" shouted Milky.

"I gotta take a leak," cried Handsome.

"Looks like there are some shops up ahead," Russo said.

Stacey snapped. "Will you guys stop acting like tourists?" She smacked me on my arm. "Will you stop looking at the ceiling, as if they were Dolly Parton's tits."

"I'll give you five dollars if you can name one of the constellations," I said.

"Fucking tourist," Stacey mumbled.

We moved away from the information station and toward the snack shops. A homeless person approached Russo.

"Got some change, my other?"

"My other?" Russo asked.

"I think he said, 'brother,' I said.

"Some change?" The homeless man pleaded.

"Yeah, here," Russo said as he dug into the pockets. "Knock yourself out." He gave the man a dollar.

"Tanks, man."

The messy man hobbled away.

"Yeah, tanks are pretty cool," Russo said jokingly.

Milky laughed. "He said 'thanks,' you ass bite."

Stacey smacked Russo's arm. "You can't be doing that."

"What?"

"If another one sees you giving out money, they'll all be asking you for change. They can tell you're not from the city."

"The dude is obviously homeless," Milky said.

"Oh my, Milky. Don't you know, you're in the fancy city," Russo said sarcastically.

"Jesus hardcore Christ! You guys are driving me insane!" Stacey snapped.

Russo puts his arm around her and said, "You're such a sensitive flatlander."

"I seriously need to use the bathroom," Handsome said with distress.

Stacey and Handsome trotted off to the rest rooms while Milky, Russo and I entered a snack shop.

An Indian American girl, who seemed to be the same age as us, was working the register. She smiled at me. She wore a white shirt with red lettering that read: I LOVE NEW YORK. She had wonderful eyes that looked like a glass of iced tea in the sun.

A slick looking suit and tie guy plopped his diet coke and newspaper on the small counter. He looked like some lousy stockbroker. At least he was conscious of his sugar and calorie intake, I thought.

The "The One Thing" by INXS played on the little FM radio near the counter.

After she rang up the suit and tie guy, she turned up the volume. Stocking magazine on the shelf near the coolers was an older woman, probably her mother. "Latika! Turn it down."

Under those gorgeous eyebrows, Latika rolled her eyes and lowered the volume. They must own the shop, I thought.

As we walked to the beverage coolers, Milky grabbed a strawberry Yoo-hoo out of the cooler and stared at it with strange curiosity. "Hey, Bailey. Have you ever had one of these?"

"Just chocolate flavor for me, sweetie."

"What about you?" Milky said to Russo.

"That shit gives me diarrhea," Russo said as he juggled a bottle of lime-flavored Gatorade. "I stick to the basics."

The mother barked at Russo. "Hey, you! Buy it or put it back!"

"What the hell?" Russo said to himself.

We stood in line to pay for the drinks.

"I got it," said Milky as he pulled out his wallet.

What a good man, I thought.

As we exited the shops, I saw Stacey and Handsome returning from the bathrooms.

"Where's my drink?" Handsome asked, as if Milky was his butler.

"Get a job." Milky said.

"Come on, we gotta catch the 6 train," Stacey said.

Again, we followed Stacey.

I looked back at Latika. She smiled as we made eye contact. Who knew if I would ever see her again?

The sounds of Grand Central faded as we walked down two flights of grimy stairs to catch the 6 train.

We reached the bottom and stood in line to buy subway tokens. After we passed through the turn stop, we walked out to the platform with the rest of the travelers.

In the distance, I could hear a subway storming along. It sounded like an amplified salad spinner.

I leaned against one of the pillars and pulled out my crushed pack of smokes. The air was stale and smelled of burning oil. I lit a disheveled cigarette and took a long drag, closing my eyes with delight. My first cigarette since Burghville, and it tasted like paradise.

I wiped the sweat from my forehead and looked at the trash near the tracks.

There were cigarette butts, crushed coffee containers and receipts, among other things, reminding me of The Tundra.

Behind me were the posters for the musicals *The Phantom of the Opera* and *Cats*.

Down the platform a bit, I saw the poster for the movie *GoodFellas*. I walked toward it for a closer look. Robert De Niro, Joe Pesci and Ray Liotta were dressed in expensive suits. Their arms were folded, and their faces looked mean and cross. Below them was a dead body lying under a subway trestle. It looked like a good movie, I thought.

A lot of gangster pictures were released in 1990. For me, the last great mobster picture was *The Untouchables*. I am not that wild about Kevin Costner, but I did like his performance in that movie. And you can never strike out with Sean Connery!

I heard a subway approaching. I moved closer to the tracks to see the train stopping along the platform across from us. It was the train running uptown.

Within moments the train departed and all was quiet again.

I took another drag of my cigarette and looked down at the tracks leading into the ominous tunnel. The way the tracks curved into the blackness made me feel anxious. I started to think about my trip to college. In two days, I would be boarding the plane for the west coast. I hated not knowing what was around the corner. But it was all in my mind.

Russo approached me and lit a cigarette. "Man, I don't know how these city people do it," he said as he fanned himself. "So, what's up with Handsome and Stacey?"

"What?"

"You know."

"What are you talking about?"

"Like he didn't tell you."

"I don't know what you're talking about," I said.

"He's been following her around like a dog in heat."

I didn't say anything.

"So, he didn't tell you," Russo said.

I looked at Milky, Stacey and Handsome chatting away down at the other end of the platform. I was a terrible liar. But I had to keep Handsome's secret safe. "No," I replied.

Russo laughed. "You mean, he didn't tell you about this." He mimicked a blow job.

I faked a gasp and said, "For real?" In the distance, the train was heard approaching.

"But we don't believe him," Russo said as he stomped out his cigarette. "I mean, if you knew about it, then maybe we would."

I started thinking that Handsome had lied to me. But why should I care?

I looked at the lights of the approaching train. People were moving to the edge of the platform. I crushed my cigarette on the pillar and followed Russo down the platform to meet Stacey, Handsome and Milky. The train stopped. There was a pause. Then the doors slid open as a bunch of people quickly exited.

We boarded the train.

Stacey found a seat for two at the back of the train.

Handsome went to sit next to her, but Russo beat him.

"You're an ass!" Handsome shouted.

Russo put his arm around Stacey and stuck his tongue out at Handsome.

"Poser," Handsome said to Russo.

"Step away from the door," said the voice over the loud-speaker.

There was a quick beeping sound.

Milky and I grabbed the bar as the doors shut. Handsome walked toward us. The subway jolted as Handsome fell into a heavy-set woman. We all laughed.

Seeing Handsome falling into the stomach of the woman reminded me of how we first met him during the first year of high school which was the tenth grade.

It was an early fall morning. Handsome was standing with the smokers (that would have been us) even though he didn't smoke. He was wearing his infamous jean jacket that featured many pins of small or unknown bands.

Handsome loved the staple bands of the late eighties, you know, Metallica, Iron Maiden, and so on. But it was damn pins of unknown bands that drew attention to himself.

Back then, the rock pins we wore on our jackets were a big deal. Maybe they still are. Who knows?

Anyway, Handsome's display of unknown bands came with jokes and jabs from dumb metalheads. Paulie Tucci was one of them.

Paulie was not the shiniest apple on the tree. I'll even take it one step farther: he was the rotten apple that fell off the tree and was eaten by insects.

One morning, before classes started, Paulie pointed to Handsome's Saxon pin, the great band from England, and said, "Saxon sucks, and so does your mother!" He then said, like a poet, "Saxon sounds like Exxon, and so does your mother, brother!"

These smaller bands were a big part of Handsome's identity. so he responded: "Tucci sounds like a putrid ass, and you suck ass!"

Everyone in Paulie's immediate family was tall, including him. In fact, my brother had gone to school with one of his brothers who played center on the high school basketball team.

Refusing to be attacked by bad poetry, Paulie moved into Handsome's space, towering over him. He ripped the Saxon pin off of his jacket and held it up in front of Handsome's blue eyes and said: "Say bye bye!"

Paulie threw the pin across the yard. The pin twirled in the air until it hit Russo in the back of his head.

Angered by the sting of the metal cylinder, Russo grabbed the pin from the cement.

"Who the fuck threw the Saxon pin?" Russo yelled.

Paulie pointed to Handsome and said, "This poser fuck!"

Russo approached Handsome and gently handed him the pin. "Fucking Saxon," he said. "They're one of those European metal bands."

"Barnsley, England, to be exact," Handsome said.

"I love their drummer," Russo said.

From there on, Handsome hung out with our group. And from a far, Paulie continued to make fun of Handsome's pins.

Then one day Paulie got a girlfriend. Shortly after that, he got her pregnant. And that was that.

Now, as the subway moved quickly, the street numbers went down and down as we moved along.

A bunch of people got off at 23rd Street. From here, we were able to sit.

Stacey stood. "You ready?"

The train began to slow.

Through the window, a sign said: BLEECKER STREET.

"Is this it?" Russo asked.

"Yeah," Stacey answered.

The train stopped as we all stood. The doors opened as we exited the train.

Russo rubbed Handsome's head and said, "You know I love you."

We exited through the turn stop and headed up the stairs.

CHAPTER 9

Bleecker Street and The Bowery

We marched up the stairs that led us from the 6 train onto the busy streets of Soho. For better or worse, we had made it to the Lower East side.

We took a moment of silence to digest the city. There was a lot of energy surrounding us, a vibrant feeling that seemed to perpetuate the mood of the atmosphere.

It was hotter in the city then it was in Burghville. I felt bad watching Milky walk the streets wearing jeans—sweating like a mad man only to hide the scar that ran down his left leg.

We all gathered at the corner of Broadway and Bleecker. Behind us, yellow cabs and delivery trucks crawled along Broadway. It was close to two o'clock and we were starving.

"Food! Food! Food!" Russo demanded.

"Is there a McDonalds close by?" Handsome asked.

"McDonalds? Are you cursed?" Stacey glowered. "You're a foot and half from the best food in the world."

"And the best pizza parlors in the world," I added.

"Pizza sounds like a plan," Milky said.

"We're going to Ray's Pizza Parlor," Stacey said leading the way.

As we followed her, I could see the tops of the two World Trade Center. Stacey nudged me and said, "Put your head down, Jimmy. You look like a–"

We all shouted: "Tourist!"

"Assholes," Stacey muttered to herself.

We all laughed as we strolled down Bleeker Street.

I put my arm around Stacey as she cracked a smile. It had been a while since I'd seen her smile.

At the pizza parlor, we packed around a small table near the window that faced Bleecker Street.

We quickly gobbled up the large pie and guzzled down our drinks like warriors returning from war. Stacey was right, it was the best pizza we had ever had.

As I chomped on some pizza crust, Milky and Russo spoke band politics, as if they were two old rich guys at a fancy country club.

"You're crazy. We'll never find a bass player if we throw out Crazy Pete," Milky said.

"What are you talking about? We're like the biggest band in the Hudson Valley," Russo said.

"I'm not denying that our band has gotten bigger. And yeah, we could probably find another bassist. But Crazy Pete can play the changes."

"Oh, come on... that's a lame excuse!" Russo snapped.

"You don't know, because you don't write the songs. Our music is complicated."

"I think Russo is right," Handsome interjected. "Crazy Pete is a fuck up and you guys would be better off without him."

Russo and Milky looked at each other for a long moment, then continued talking, ignoring Handsome's comment.

Russo said, "I met this kid at our last show, and he said—"

"Here's a caveat to your lively bass player debate," Stacey said. "Your songs are too long, metal is going out the door, and you should rethink your futures."

Russo kicked Stacey's chair and said, "Don't forget, you met us at a Dead and Gone show. I mean, what would you have done if you never met us?" Russo looked at me and shot me a wink and a smile.

Stacey dramatically fell into my arms. "My god! What would have I done? I would have been lost and in the sauce if I didn't meet the great and wonderful Dead and Gone."

Russo turned to Milky. "Getting back to Crazy Pete—"

"Okay. Enough of the band talk," I said.

"Yes, I think we've all had enough of Milky and Russo's chit, chat, chit chat," Stacey said, miming her hand like an alligator.

"Whatever." Russo tossed his tomato-stained napkin onto the table. "I guess some of us already have their plans in check."

Russo could not go anywhere without talking about the band. He was too worried about popularity rather than the art of making music.

Milky was the heart and force of the band, which gave him the most power. Russo knew this but could never say it.

"Come on, let's get out of here," Handsome said.

We were eager to venture around the lower east side. And with that, we headed back into the heat and Bleeker Street.

"Anyone in the mood for a Strawberry Yoo-hoo?" Milky enticingly asked.

"What is up with you and the strawberry Yoo-hoo?" I asked.

"I'm a man with a plan, Sir James."

"Yes, somebody please tell me the plan. I'm dying out here," Russo said, fanning himself.

"The show starts in about an hour or so. Let's walk around," Stacey said.

"Are there any good record stores?" Russo asked.

"No," Stacey said sarcastically.

Russo shrugged.

"What do you think? Of course there are great record stores. In fact, we're very close to Bleeker Bob's," Stacey said.

"Well, that's where I'm heading," Handsome said.

"What are you going to buy?" Milky asked. "You have no money, you jobless jokester."

"I'm going to find a thrift shop. Does anyone wanna come?" Stacey asked.

We all said, "No."

"Come on! You geeks!"

"I'll go with you," I said.

Russo chuckled and said, "Yeah, Jimmy. Go buy a red wig and some bell bottoms. It's on me!"

"Where's the record store?" Handsome asked.

"Go up to Thompson and make a right. It's on Third Avenue, you'll see it around the corner," Stacey said.

"So basically Third Ave is parallel with Bleecker?" Milky said.

"Basically, you're a smart person, Robert," she said.

"Where should we meet?" Russo asked.

"CBGB is at the end of Bleeker Street. You can't miss it. We'll meet up around three," she said.

Russo looked at Handsome and Milky and asked, "Who's got a watch?"

"What difference does it make?" Milky answered.

***

Stacey tapped her foot as I tied my shoelace. I don't know how she could walk in those black Doc Martins, I thought.

"Come on, James. We don't want to be late."

I made the last loop and stood.

As we trucked along Bleeker Street, I could smell Stacey's armpits. The smell didn't bother me, though. In a strange way, I kind of liked it. It made her human—the stench of body odor piecing through her punk rock persona she had momentarily taken on.

But I could not stop thinking about what Handsome had shared with me last night.

He must be lying, I thought.

"Are you having fun?" she asked.

"It's not so bad," I said.

"It's New York City. It's the best place in the world!"

"I certainly know," I said, projecting with the next question. "So how did you convince Handsome to cut his hair?"

"He suggested it, not me," she said defensively.

"Yeah, right."

"He asked me to clip him, so I clipped his hair. Besides, his hair looks better wearing it short."

"Are you ever going to grow back your hair?" I asked.

"You think I'm ugly now?"

"No, I just think you have nice hair."

"I'm no longer that metal girl you still dream about, James."

We could not find the thrift shop that Stacey spoke so highly of. Instead, we popped into an antique shop.

Inside, I instantly sensed it was a great one. The good ones were always messy and smelled musty. The man behind the counter, who wore a Hawaiian short sleeved button up shirt, smiled and said to Stacey, "Cute haircut, sweetheart."

Stacey and I slowly walked along the aisle. Each booth was unique and geared to a certain theme. I stopped at one that had mostly movie memorabilia. I grabbed an old 8mm camera and pointed it at her. "Let's see those teeth."

She flipped me the middle finger and said, "Get that phallic looking lens out of my face."

"Am I sensing some film psychoanalysis?"

"Yeah. You're a psycho," Stacey said.

"*Psycho*. The great horror film by Sir Alfred Hitchcock."

"Never seen it."

I put down the camera with disbelief. "You've never saw *Psycho*?"

"I've seen the shower scene, so I pretty much seen the best part of the movie."

"You gotta see the whole thing through. There's this scene—"

"Check that out," Stacey said pointing.

It was a poster for the movie, *Giant*. The poster, which was encased in a glass frame, featured a sultry sky with the title superimposed in red lettering *GIANT*. Toward the bottom of the poster was a picture of James Dean, Elizabeth Taylor, and Rock Hudson.

"Look at the price," Stacey said.

The sticker said $250.00.

"It says it's an original poster." Stacey looked at me. "Have you ever seen this movie?"

"Yeah. It was James Dean's last movie."

"Did you like it?"

"It was one of those films where it plays better in your mind after you have watched it, if that makes any sense at all."

"Like good memories," she said.

We browsed through the rest of the store. I stopped at a booth that was crowded with a bunch of postcards.

I flipped through them and found an old one of Burghville. I couldn't believe it. I've never seen a postcard of Burghville. Not like I had been searching for one!

The postcard was a grand picture of the Hudson Valley. It showd the Hudson River flowing toward the foreground, engulfing much of the picture.

Toward the left of the frame, was an image of two docked ferries. In the background, to the left, was an image of the riverbanks and the city itself. Against the horizon were the two chapels pricking the blue sky.

Nature, transportation and religion, all rolled into this small postcard.

I could not read the postmark and guessed it was from the turn of the century given that the bridges were not in the picture.

The letter on the flipside of the postcard was faded and hard to read. The only thing I could make out from the elaborate cursive writing was: WE WILL STILL HAVE THOSE MEMORIES.

The postcard was a mystery. *Who could have sent it?*

"Hey, Stacey. Check this out." She approached me as I showed her the postcard.

"What is this?" She then took the postcard from my hand. Her eyes furrowed as she handed it back to me. "Oh God, James. You're so sentimental."

I shrugged and then proceeded to the checkout counter and bought it for two dollars.

I shoved the postcard in my pocket as we exited the antique shop.

We walked east along Bleeker, which led us directly to the Bowery. As we reached the end of the street, directly across from us was a crowd of kids gathered near the white awning.

The red lettering on the awning read: CBGB. Parked near it were a couple of beat-up vans

Stacey jumped up and down. "I'm so excited!"

The club was much smaller than what I had seen in the magazines. I was expecting something grand for such a legendary place.

We crossed Bowery and moved in with the rest of the crowd.

It seemed like everyone had a shaved head. It was a different vibe than the metal crowd. I saw no one with long hair.

In the sticky heat, they fashioned jeans and black Doc Martins. They wore Token Entry, Minor Threat, Sick of it All, Cro Mags, and Bad Brains shirts. Some even wore punk shirts like The Buzzcocks, The Ramones, Sex Pistols, and The Clash.

Some sat in circles on the pavement.

Some leaned against the lamp post.

A few girls had shaved heads just like Stacey.

Next to the club was an old hotel. There were eccentric and animated people conversing outside it. Everyone seemed calm and happy, smoking their cigarettes in the bowels of the Bowery.

Stacey's eyes widened as an old blue van pulled up near the white awning.

"They're here! They're here!"

She rushed over to the van as the members of F.U. stepped out. Mike was the last one out as Stacey ran to him.

I was surprised to see he had shaved his head. He looked a lot cleaner with short hair. Maybe Handsome was right; we'll all have shaved heads soon!

I never had any gripes with Mike. We had the same English class in the eleventh grade—and we had some cool conversations about music. Though, I had never thought he would be interested in Stacey.

Stacey hugged him, then kissed him on the lips. I wondered if she would acknowledge that I came with her.

I could easily walk up to Mike and give him a friendly "hello," but I wanted to see if she would wave me over.

She grabbed one of the guitar cases and went inside with the rest of the band, leaving me by myself.

I looked around to see if the guys were in sight. *Maybe they had gotten lost?*

With no one to talk to, I sat on the sidewalk, reached into my shorts and lit a cigarette.

I pulled out my postcard of Burghville and stared at it for a moment and then fanned myself with it.

The feeling shooting through me felt familiar

August 18
Doors Open at
3pm

Hardcore Matinee at
CBGB
315 Bowery at Bleeker

Stomach Virus

with

Unchecked
Stains

A
New
World
Order

F.U.
(From Upstate NY)

August 18
Doors Open at 3pm

CHAPTER 10

Where's the Unity?

"Hey, Bailey!" I looked up and saw Milky, Handsome and Russo approaching northward from the Bowery.

I quickly stood. "What happened?"

Handsome threw his hands up with dismay and shouted, "What do you think?"

Russo nodded to Milky with his thumb. "This psychopath wanted another strawberry Yoo-hoo. We went looking for a store and got lost!"

"I hope it tasted good," I said to Milky.

"Bliss, my friend! Bliss!"

Handsome anxiously looked at the crowd of kids.

"Look all you want, she went into the club with Mike and the rest of F.U.," I said.

"I'm not looking for Stacey."

"She left you out here by yourself?" Milky said.

"That's messed up!" Russo snapped.

"It hasn't been that bad. I've been watching this weird, old lady that keeps jogging up and down the Bowery and counting each time she goes by." And at that moment, she came jogging southward. "Look! Her she comes now!"

None of the kids in front of CBGB acknowledged her presence as she jogged through the crowd. She was a confused ghost ship sailing along the lonely seas.

"That's number eight," I said.

"She must be local," Milky said.

"More like a loco," Handsome joked.

Russo sized up the scene. "Man, I thought CBGB was a lot bigger."

"Ditto that," I said.

"This is what the scene is like," Handsome said. "There's no glamour or commercialization—it's all for real."

"What are you talking about? This is welfare rock," Russo said.

Handsome said, "Keep it low with that talk, dude. We're in the lower east side, not the plaza, you idiot."

Russo lit a cigarette. "Whatever. This shit is overrated."

I joined Russo on the hot concrete.

Russo nudged Handsome. "Aren't you going to mingle with your kind? You know? Keep it real."

"You gotta keep cool, Russo. These kids don't mess around," Handsome said softly.

"I thought there's a lot of unity in the scene?" Milky whispered.

"Fuck you," Handsome whispered back.

"That's what I thought," Milky whispered.

From inside the club we heard the repeated sound of a snare drum, then the thump of a bass drum, then the banging of toms, and then the crash of cymbals.

Russo nodded his head to the thump and said: "DRUM : CHECK : IS : A : NIGHT : MARE."

A drumbeat was finally heard.

"Ah, the perks of the opening band," Milky said.

"Good drum sound," Russo said. "Robby's drums usually sound like murder."

We heard the guitar, then the warm sound of a bass. We heard Mike say the infamous: "Check one, two. Check one, two." Within a few moments, F.U performed a song.

"I can't believe I'm going say this, but they–"

I put my hand on Russo's shoulder and whispered, "Let's not ruin the day for Milky."

Russo nodded.

After F.U. finished their song, the house music faded up. And shortly after, there was a sudden sound of claps and cheers as a line formed in front of the entrance.

"I wonder if this place has air conditioning?" Russo asked.

"Yeah, probably the best in town," I said.

We joined the queue, while the summer sun cooked us, as if we were chickens in a rotisserie oven.

Handsome tapped me on the shoulder and pointed forward. "Why are they frisking everyone?"

The man standing in front of us, turned to Handsome and said, with a strong city accent, "Last week someone got capped."

"Capped?" Handsome said with big eyes.

"Bang! Bang! Fucking shot, you know?"

Handsome looked at him with confused eyes.

The man, who looked a little older than us, wore a lemon-colored Bad Brains shirt which featured a lightning bolt striking the U.S. Capitol Building. Below it read, BANNED IN D.C. Next to him was a woman who fashioned a short black punk style hair.

"I'm surprised you guys didn't hear about it," the man said.

"We're not from around here," I said.

"Where are you guys from?"

"Burghville," Handsome said.

"Oh yeah, I know that place. Up in the Catskills."

"My name is Stanley," Handsome said.

"It's Handsome, not Stanley," Russo quickly interjected.

"Handsome? That's one fucked up nickname. You must get a lot of ass with a name like that," the man said.

The man extended his hand to Handsome and said, "I'm Dan and this is Vera."

Vera, who was wearing blood red lipstick, simply looked at us all, rolled her eyes, and turned the other way.

We each introduced ourselves. And as the line slowly moved, we talked more.

"So, you guys are here to see Stomach Virus?" Dan asked.

"Sort of. We're friends with F.U." Handsome said.

"F.U.?" Dan asked with confusion.

"They're the opening band," Handsome said.

"And they suck," Milky added.

"But you came down to see 'em?" Dan said.

Russo put his hand on my shoulder. "Bailey is leaving for film school this Monday, so we wanted to take him out before he departs for the land of sunshine."

"Our friend Stacey is dating the singer. It was actually her idea," I said.

"Gonna be hot on the west coast," Dan said.

"It's a dry heat," I said.

"You guys like hardcore?" Dan asked.

"Not really," Russo said. "We're more into thrash and speed metal. Though Milky likes the Crumbsuckers."

"Some of us like hardcore," Handsome said.

"Yeah, crossover is getting bigger and bigger. A lot of the old punk, three power chord riffs is considered old school."

"Tell me about it!" Russo said.

"You've been to a lot of shows?" I asked.

"I've seen them all." Dan pointed to his Bad Brains shirt. "Except these guys."

Dan seemed like a cool guy. He was into hardcore, but knew about other types of music, which made him stand out from the rest of the crowd. Back then, everyone was so concerned about genres. It was an anomaly to be into everything. Dan was breaking some barriers, whether he knew it or not

Soon we finally reached the door. The once muffled house music was now piercing from the doorway, skipping along into the city air. Standing before us was a bouncer, wearing sunglasses, ready to protect CBGB from the terror of youth.

"Spread your goddamn arms!" The bouncer shouted.

I focused on the bouncer's black CBGB shirt as he frisked Handsome.

"What does OMFUG mean?" Handsome asked.

"Don't fuck with me, you little son of a bitch!"

Handsome looked at him with big eyes and then shrugged.

We entered the steamy club, and each paid the woman behind the ticket counter ten dollars each. Her arm, blanketed with tattoos, extended outward and stamped our hands. We proceeded further inside.

Graffiti and band stickers of various band names decorated the walls. The stage was small and low to the crowd. We moved past the large PA speakers, which was carpeted with more band stickers. Running parallel to the right wall was a big couch, and that was where we headed. We somehow found a section to sit.

Stacey was nowhere in sight.

My eyes spotted a kid wearing a backpack, abruptly pushing his way through the crowd to the front of the stage. He had hefty sideburns, and curly black hair that was a bit long.

I nudged Milky and gestured to the kid. "How did that dude get into the club with a backpack?"

Before Milky could answer, the house lights dimmed as the house music faded. We all stood except for Milky. Everyone began to clap as F.U. took the stage. Standing off to the side of the stage was Stacey, as if she was their manager.

Mike grabbed the microphone off the stand and then wrapped the cord around his forearm like a fisherman reeling in a big mouth bass. The crowd anxiously waited for the first song.

Mike confidently shouted: "Yo, what's up New York City! We're F.U. from upstate New York."

I heard some laughter.

Mike turned toward the rest of the band and said, "Let's do it." They broke into a fast beat over open power chords. The chords were diminished and gothic sounding.

Mike jumped all over the stage like a starving ape in a steel cage.

Within a few measures of the song, they cut the beat in half as Mike began to sing, shout, or whatever you want to call it.

Stacey was jumping up and down. She looked like the band's puppy dog.

And with all the energy F.U. emitted, the crowd stayed put, with their arms folded, nodding their heads to the beat. The only real movement, besides F.U., was the cigarette smoke lingering into the red and blue stage lights, right above their equipment. But I sensed the crowd liked them.

Suddenly, the kid with the backpack slammed into the crowd like a pinball. He had his hands and legs kicking, almost like he was in a karate movie.

"Check out Bruce Lee!" Russo shouted over the music.

Milky, who was now standing behind us, said, "Let's move up."

And like idiots, we moved closer to the middle. It was even hotter in the middle, and it smelled of sweat and armpits. *All this for entertainment*, I thought.

F.U. finished their first song as the crowd clapped. While holding the microphone tightly, Mike dogged the crowd with psychotic eyes and then screamed, "One! Two! Three! Move!"

The band broke into a slow beat, as the crowd erupted. I saw the kid with backpack coming toward us. He reached behind him and retrieved a small hammer from his backpack. The crowd swayed back and forth, trying to avoid him.

Milky screamed: "Look out! We're gonna get hammered!"

The kid was running toward us like a speeding train. We quickly moved out of the way.

All four of us retreated to the couch. As the second song came to an end, Milky pushed Handsome and asked, "Where's the unity?"

The third song started. The kids were now slam dancing and stage diving. Again, I saw the kid with backpack with crashing and kicking into the crowd. No sign of the hammer.

"All this for entertainment," I yelled.

"And culture!" Milky added.

When it came to slam dancing, it didn't make a difference what scene you were a part of. Metal, hardcore, punk, it all gave violent people permission to be violent. As the crowd swayed back and forth, this girl, fell backwards onto me.

"Sorry," she said.

At least she didn't have a hammer.

The song ended.

"This is madness!" I said.

F.U. played three more songs. And then Mike said, "Thank you and goodnight." And before you know it, F.U. began breaking down their equipment. The house music turned on. Most of the crowd funneled out through the exit.

It took about ten minutes, and finally we were outside on the Bowery. Although it was ninety-something degrees in the city, the air felt refreshing compared the heat inside the club.

I checked my pocket and was surprised to see that my cigarettes had survived the malaise.

"We should get a drink before we go back in that sweat box," Russo said.

"There's a store across the street," I said.

"Come on, Handsome, let's head over," Russo said.

"Why do I have to go?" Handsome asked.

"Who's going to protect me from your unified skinhead friends?"

"Get me a strawberry Yoo-hoo!" Milky shouted.

Jogging her way through the crowd was the old lady. "There she goes again," I said.

I saw Dan and Vera making their way through the crowd in front of the club. He made eye contact with me and walked over to us. "Your friend's band is pretty good," he said genuinely.

"I can't believe I'm going to say this, but I thought they sounded okay," Milky said.

"Too bad Russo wasn't here to hear you say it," I said.

We saw the kid with backpack moving through the crowd, eyeballing each person. He looked like a bull searching for the red.

"Who's that kid?" Milky asked Dan.

Dan quickly looked at the kid and then back at us, shaking his head. "Stay away from him, man. He's fucked in the head."

"I think the hammer in the mosh pit gave away that element," I said.

"That's Billy. He's from some fucked up gang or something."

"He's nothing. He's just mad at the world because he can't identify with the phallus," Vera said.

It was the first sentence she spoke.

"Don't mind Vera. She's an English student with an emphasis in Freud. She's getting her Master's degree," Dan added with humor.

"Moshing is a lot different here then the shows I've been to," Milky said.

"Metal moshing is way different than hardcore. We don't even call it moshing, it's called dancing, because there's groove—you know? You dance to the rhythm."

"Slam dancing, moshing, dancing; it's all about the penis, the Law, the identification with the totem—the symbol of the group," Vera said. She turned to me and said, "Right?"

"Sure."

"You don't know what you're talking about. Slam dancing is a ritual," Dan said heatedly to her. "And besides women slam dance, too, you know."

"I don't know why you try to make the scene out to be like it's SO cultured and everyone is SO open minded. It's all the same," Vera said. "Screwed up kids go to metal shows and screwed up kids go to hardcore shows."

Nobody said anything.

Dan pursed his lips, then said, "We're gonna head to the store to get something drink. I'll see you guys later."

Vera and Dan walked across the Bowery, intersecting Russo and Handsome.

"There goes Stacey," Milky said.

I turned to see Stacey smoking a cigarette with Mike. Within a couple of minutes, a few kids walked up to Mike and shook his hand.

For the moment, F.U. had the spotlight on them. They went the distance. They had played New York City and lots of kids came up to them to say that they liked their music. To me it was a fantastic achievement. A band from Burghville was making headway.

Of course, I would never speak positively about F.U. in front of Milky and Russo. Even though Milky held his pride about hating them, I knew he could handle seeing them gain attention. But for Russo, I could feel the heat of Russo's envy when F.U. took the stage.

Handsome and Russo came back with plenty of drinks.

I watched Russo chug down half of his soda. "You should be drinking water. Soda will make you thirstier," I joked.

Russo burped. "Water tastes like dog vomit. And I don't drink dog vomit."

"Who's playing next?" Milky asked.

"I heard someone say Unchecked Stains," Handsome replied.

"With a sweet name like that, they better be good," Russo said.

"What did you think of F.U.?" Handsome asked Russo.

"Look who's come to join us," Russo said, avoiding Handsome's question.

Stacey strolled over to us, as if she owned the block. "What do you upstate metalheads think so far?"

"I'm feeling very cultured," Milky said in a high brow manner.

"Don't believe the hype," Russo said.

"Oh, knock it off," she said.

"It's hot as balls in there!" Milky said.

"You guys are a bunch of tourists."

"I think we need a new insult," I offered.

The kids were lining up at the door.

"I have a good feeling about Unchecked Stains," Milky said.

We ended up near the big couch again. Stacey stood with us. Mike and the wonderful members of F.U. might have told her to hit the high road, while still leaving the question open: *Was she still dating Mike?*

The lights dimmed as everyone clapped and whistled. Suddenly Beethoven was heard over the loudspeaker as Unchecked Stains took the stage.

They were a four-piece band and looked like they were in their mid-forties and worked in construction. I could not keep my eyes off the singer.

He was bald and a bit overweight. He wore a pair of blue jeans that seemed too tight on him.

He took off his shirt, revealing a large tattoo of a cobra snake across his chest. He wiped his arm pits with the shirt and then threw it out into the crowd. Beethoven ended.

The drummer gave a four count with his drumsticks and broke into an upbeat song.

The singer's voice was as thunderous as a midnight storm. He bobbled back and forth along the stage, raising his hands in anger like a man who was fired from his beloved job.

He belted out a few lines with bravado.

During the chorus, he would stick the microphone into the crowd.

A pile of kids jumped and grabbed hold of the microphone and shout the chorus of the song.

Suddenly the guitarist strummed an open chord while the drums dropped out.

The guitarist let the note resonate until the sound became feedback. Just when he had everyone's attention, his hand slid down the neck of the guitar and then jammed into a slow and grinding riff.

In a couple of measures, the drums and bass joined in with a slow tempo.

The crowd moshed to the beat. But it was not moshing; it was like dancing. I had never seen a crowd move with rhythm. They all knew the slow riff. They had been waiting for it. I've never felt such energy. Unchecked Stains knew how to work the crowd. The song ended as everyone erupted with cheers and whistles, myself included.

"Boo Hoo!" The singer shouted back at the crowd. "Your joy means nothing to me!" He burped, then added, "I could care less about the hardcore scene!" The crowd laughed and clapped.

We all looked at each other and laughed.

"I wish he was our high school commencement speaker," Milky said.

The singer seemed to enjoy berating and hectoring the crowd before and after each song.

Unchecked Stains pounded out song after song. They were unique and had a style of music I had never heard. Their roots seemed to be embedded in Black Sabbath and Slayer.

I was fascinated that the crowd would jump on stage during certain parts of the song and sing along with the singer, even if he pushed one of them off the stage.

I couldn't make out what the singer was saying, but there appeared to be substance in his lyrics. And even though the singer appeared to hate everyone, his songs (in a strange way) seemed personal.

The singer said, "I hope you are having fun because soon you'll all be in the fucking Middle East with sun burns."

I was taken aback that he was referring to Iraq's invasion of Kuwait that had happened a few weeks ago.

The singer held up a long sleeve black T-shirt to the crowd. In red lettering was the name of the band, UN-CHECKED STAINS.

"Who wants a nice T-shirt?" The singer asked enticingly.

He began wiping his big sweaty belly with the shirt. He then stuck the shirt down his pants as the crowd moaned with disgust. "Here you go, you losers." He threw the soiled shirt out into the crowd. "This is our last song."

They broke into a slow beat and then the guitar and bass joined in as the crowd went into a frenzy. Within moments a fight broke out. Strangely, the kid with the backpack was not involved.

The crowd swayed back and forth as the bouncers threw the culprits out.

And a few minutes later, the song was over, and Unchecked Stains were off the sweaty, stage.

The house music turned on as we headed outside.

"I'm dying," Russo said in pain.

Back onto the street, the sun was edging closer to the horizon and the air was still. The city felt more active as the sky got darker. I felt trouble was in the air, but I tried not to focus on it.

We sat on the pavement, trying to recap what we had just witnessed.

"Those guys were great!" I said.

"I don't think so," Russo said.

"Come on! That singer was nuts!" I said.

"Why did he bring up Middle East?" Handsome asked.

Milky rubbed his chin as he became upset. "Don't you know what's going on over there?"

Handsome was not good at keeping on top of current events—particularly the required details necessary to have a conversation with Milky.

"You need to watch the news." Milky said. "It's a big deal."

"I really liked the singer," I said to prevent Milky from going into a tirade about the news media.

"He was disgusting," a girl's voice said.

We turned around and saw that Stacey had followed us out.

"You know, he practically destroyed the room backstage," Stacey said. She sat in between Handsome's legs. "You got a smoke?"

"Sure," Handsome said as he pulled out a pack of cigarettes.

I couldn't take it anymore. I was so fed up with her fakery.

"I'm heading to the store," I said.

"I'll come with you," Milky said.

We quickly crossed the Bowery.

Before we went inside the store, Milky asked, "What's wrong, Jimmy?"

I don't know why I said it, but I did. "Stacey, she's a goddamn whore!"

She wasn't. And I knew it.

Then I thought about Handsome's secret and was about share it with Milky. But I didn't

154

"Come on. Let's get something drink."

Inside, I grabbed a couple of waters. By now, you can probably guess what Milky bought. We paid the man behind the register and headed back onto the Bowery.

Most of the kids in front of CBGB were gone. As we walked across the Bowery, we saw Russo, Handsome and Stacey were nowhere in sight.

"Where did they go?" Milky asked with urgency.

"Hopefully in the club," I said while sticking the extra water in my pocket.

Milky drank his Strawberry Yoo-hoo in a few gulps. We greeted the big man at the club's entrance.

Milky raised his hand to show the man his stamp.

After he checked Milky, he looked at the bulge in my pocket.

"What's in your pocket?" the bouncer said to me.

I pulled out the water.

He took it from me. "No drinks in the club."

I showed him my stamp.

"Go ahead," he said.

Stomach Virus was already on stage. We squeezed through the crowd to the big couch. There was still no sign of Russo and Handsome. The crowd was out of control. Stomach Virus was tearing the place apart. Their songs were short and to the point. By the time we reached the couch, they had played two songs.

Milky turned to me. "I don't see them.

"What do we do?"

Milky shrugged.

Stomach Virus's songs were kind of punk sounding. And they had what I called those "middle slam dance riffs." Slam dancing was indeed a world apart from the metal world. Dan was right. Slam dancing had groove and rhythm.

These bands may never be mainstream. But who wanted them to be popular?

The scene presented personal expression. The lyrics the band sang had meaning within.

Maybe it was the reason why everyone jumped on stage and chanted the chorus with the singer. There was no barrier between the band and the audience. It seemed to be the essence of the hardcore scene.

Suddenly, my body was propelled into the backs of a few punk girls.

I quickly turned to see Milky face to face with a punk kid, who fashioned a blue Mohawk and white tee shirt emblazoned with the name, INCH BY INCH.

Milky pushed the punk kid, causing him to topple over his friends.

Just as I went to grab Milky, the bouncer yanked him from behind and quickly escorted him out the door.

The bouncer left a clear path behind, so it was easy for me to exit the club.

"He started it, not me!" Milky yelled at the bouncer with frustration.

"This ain't elementary school. Now get the fuck out of here!" The bouncer hollered.

I intervened. "Come on, Milky. Let's get out of here before they come after us."

We ran across the Bowery and headed northward. I looked back and saw the kid with the Mohawk and a few of his friends patrolling in front of the club, looking for two upstate kids.

"I think we're cool," I said.

We continued northward on Bleeker.

"What happened?" I asked.

"He thought I grabbed his girlfriends' ass! I just bumped into her."

"Anything can happen when you're packed like sardines!" I said.

Milky's eyes scanned the street and the buildings while rubbing his chin. "You know how to get back to Grand Central?"

I shrugged.

Milky laughed. "Whose idea was it to go to the city?"

"I don't know. But that person should be locked up."

"There's got to be a subway stop along Bleeker," Milky said.

I wasn't anxious. I knew Milky and I were smart enough to find our way home.

Looking northward, I could see the halos created by the city lights above the buildings. And further on, the sky was getting dark. Large jets zoomed overhead. Police sirens sang in the distance.

I was thinking about Russo and Handsome, wondering how they would get home, when Milky said, "I've been thinking about quitting the band."

That took me by surprise. "What brought this on?" I asked.

"I'm just tired of playing this type of music. Plus, I'm sick of Burghville. I just want to leave, go somewhere else. And Russo! He's got this manifesto on how big we're going to be. I never saw myself as a rock star. I joined the band to have fun. You know what I mean?"

Milky just confessed what I had always known. And I was happy to hear him say the words.

But I couldn't help thinking why he did not apply for college, especially if he was planning to quit the band. Yet there was one thing I knew about Milky. I said to him: "You can do anything you want."

He smiled as he put his sweaty arm around me. "Maybe I'll go to California with you."

We walked a few more blocks while smoking and talking. Our ears were suddenly drawn to the sound of jazz in the distance.

We headed toward the sound, leading us to a café.

A bunch of people were sitting under an awning. I knew nothing about jazz music, but I did know Soho was a great place to hear it.

Jammed into the corner of the small restaurant was the band. The smooth bass rhythm and the thin sound of the ride cymbal made me feel relaxed.

Milky pointed forward, "Check it out."

We saw the steps leading down to a subway terminal. On the sign was the number 6 encased in a green circle.

"I wonder which one will take us to Grand Central," Milky asked.

"Excuse me," a girl's voice said.

We both turned and saw two girls who looked to be the same age as us.

I was drawn to the one girl in the sun yellow dress. Her hair was bobbed, and she wore thin black glasses. She asked, "Are you guys heading to Grand Central?"

The other girl, who had both hands in the back pockets of her jean shorts, smiled.

"Yeah," Milky said.

"We're heading there, too. Come on. We'll show you the way," the girl with the jean shorts said.

"Sweet!" Milky said as we followed them. "I'm Milky and this is Jimmy."

"I'm Kelly," The girl with black glasses said.

"And I'm Laura," the one with the jean shorts said.

"Where are you heading to?" I asked.

"Hartford, Connecticut,' Kelly said. "That's where I go to college."

"Is this your first semester?"

"Sophomore," Kelly replied.

"What about you?" Laura asked me.

"I'm a freshman."

"What school?"

"UCLA"

"West coast. Wow! It's going to be hot out there."

I didn't bother telling her it was a dry heat.

We continued to talk as we headed down the steps to the 6 train.

I completely forgot that we lost Russo and Handsome.

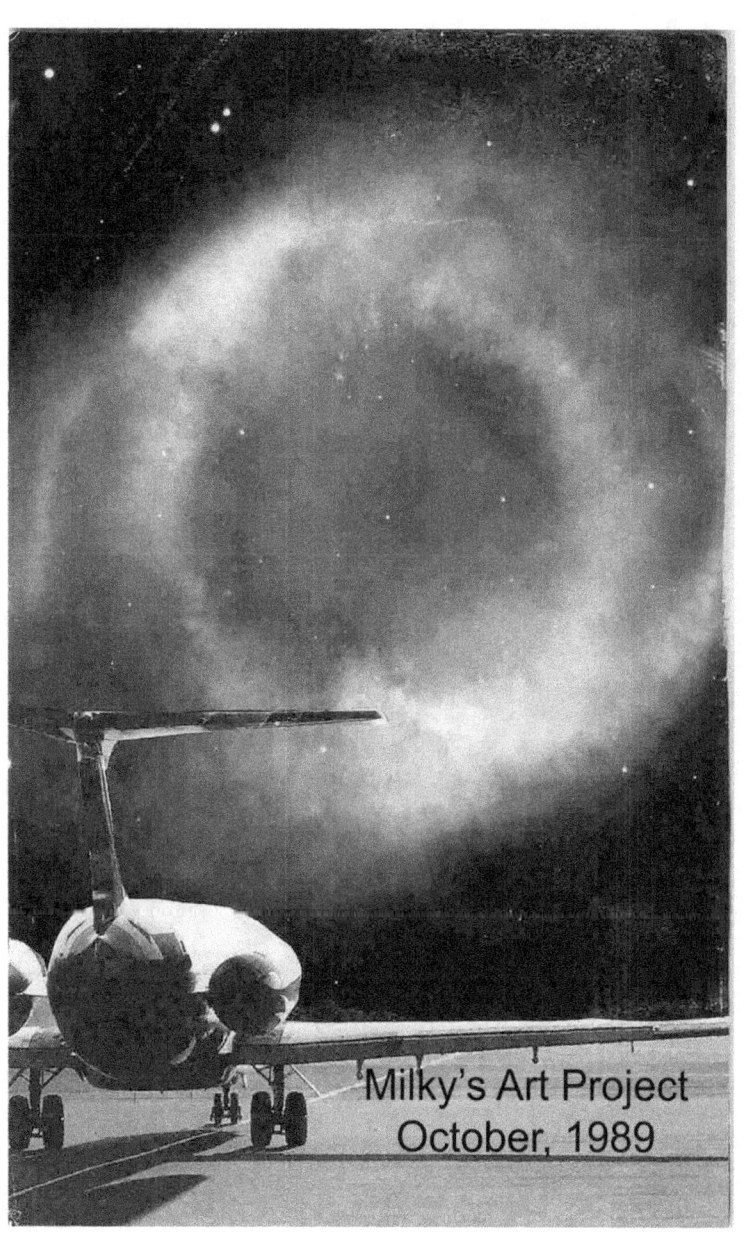

Milky's Art Project
October, 1989

CHAPTER 11

Milky's Departure

As we walked down the steps to the subway platform, the ambience of the city drifted away like a mustang galloping off into a cream-colored sunset.

We reached the bottom of the stairs, inhaling the smell of oil.

"Allow me, my friends," Milky said as he bought us each a subway token.

"Thank you," Laura said.

As Milky handed me the token, I whispered, "Good move."

We proceeded through the turn stop and out onto the boarding platform.

I heard a subway approaching as the floor rumbled.

The train reached the platform, bringing with it a gush of warm air. The silver doors opened as people scuttled out.

We boarded the train and quickly found some empty seats. Kelly and I sat near the doors while Milky and Laura sat across from us. The air released from the train's brakes as the subway howled.

"What brings you guys to the city?" Laura asked.

"It's a long story. But to be quick, Jimmy is leaving for college on Monday, so we decided to take him out for one more hurrah."

"Who's 'all we'?" Kelly asked.

"We came to the city with some other friends," Milky said.

"We lost our friends at CBGB's," I added.

"What bands did you see?" Laura asked.

"Ones that bring hammers into the mosh pit," Milky said.

Milky and Laura broke off into their own conversation.

Kelly turned to me, "They have a great film and theater program at UCLA. Is that what you're going to study?"

"How did you guess?"

"Just a lucky feeling. So, how did you get in? I heard it's competitive."

"I submitted some of my photos and a couple of papers I wrote on Stanley Kubrick."

"I like Kubrick. *2001*," she said." What a great movie."

The subway slowed, then came to a halt.

"Check this out," I said pointing to the subway doors. She looked at doors.

I then said, "Open the pod doors, Hal."

The subway doors opened as some passengers exited.

Dumb joke, but we laughed.

"What are you studying at Hartford?" I asked.

"Music."

"No way! What instrument?"

"Piano."

"That's cool," I said.

She laughed and then said, "My father once told me that he knew a guy who got a degree in music and is now cleaning toilets at some technology plant."

"I wouldn't worry about that. My father is the same way about me going into film. But I don't care."

The train began to slow as we approached the stop for Astor Place. The doors opened and people departed and boarded—nothing too exciting.

"Milky and my friend Russo have a band back home."

"Really?"

"Maybe I should rephrase that. They had a band. Milky is quitting but hasn't announced it yet."

"What instrument does he play?" she asked.

"Guitar," I said. "He's got perfect pitch."

"The sound of this subway is in the key of G," Milky said, overhearing us.

The subway doors shut as we moved along.

"What's the name of their band?" Kelly asked.

"Dead and Gone."

"I'm nervous to ask what kind of music they play."

"Speed metal," I said.

"I have some friends in our department who are into that music. There is this one kid who wrote his thesis on Cliff Burton," she said.

"I truly believe that Metallica will never be the same without Cliff," I said.

"Cliff rules," a random passenger, who was wearing a *Twilight Zone* T-shirt, said.

"What kind of music do you like?" I asked her.

"I'll pretty much listen to anything. But I gotta say, there's no exciting bands these days."

"I know what you mean. The music scene is so messed up. I mean, the bands on the top ten charts are mostly crap. There's no one making waves like the Stones or The Beatles did back in the sixties. But I'm sure some band will come along and change everything."

The train began to slow down as we reached the stop for Grand Central.

Milky had his arm around Laura. Like I said, it was that quick for him. It was still strange to see him intimate with a girl. He never talked about sex or what girls he thought were beautiful. Russo and Handsome, on the other hand, like to describe all the details. Sometimes a little too detailed.

We departed the train and headed for the stairs.

Kelly stopped to tie her sneakers. She then leaned up as a snippet of her black hair fell across her face, shadowing her round visage.

I gently grabbed the strip of her soft hair and pulled it behind her ear. She smiled at me. It felt right.

There was something comforting about her.

I loved her sneakers and summer dress. I admired the way she crossed her legs and leaned forward when I talked.

Wish I had one more day.

We moved along with the throng of people to the stairs, then proceeded to the ticket booths at Grand Central.

The little shop where Latika worked was closed.

Through the arched windows I could see the sky was turning black.

The energy at Grand Central I had felt about eight hours ago was tense and unpredictable.

I was unsure if it was safe to be at the station at night.

Who was there to ask? Stacey? I was a tourist, remember?

I stopped by the information booth and grabbed a schedule.

"What time is your train?" Laura asked us.

Milky looked at the clock above the information booth. "I think we just missed ours. What about you guys?" Milky.

"We can hang out until your train comes," Laura said.

"You want to get something to eat?" Milky asked Laura.

"Sure," she said said with big eyes.

While Laura and Milky took off, Kelly turned to me and asked, "You like coffee?"

"I live and die by coffee."

We found a Dunkin Donuts and grabbed two coffees—cream, sugar and all. We sat near the entrance for the Metro North platform.

"It's funny how fast Laura and Milky connected," I said.

"Here's something funnier," she said. "We saw you two and your friends earlier."

"No way!"

"Yeah, we saw you all eating at the pizza parlor this afternoon."

"Even in New York City, it's a small world," I said.

"Who was the girl you were with?"

"Oh, that's Stacey. She's just a friend."

"Four guys and a girl. That's interesting," she said.

A quiet a moment came over us.

"And the funny thing is that I didn't even want to come to the city," I said.

"Why did you come?"

I wanted to tell Kelly that my trip was more like a mission. I wanted to see Handsome fall on his face.

But the more I thought about it, the more I realized coming to the city was not about Handsome. It was about someone else.

I was leaving in a few days. But why did it matter so much to me? What would I have gained? I happened to meet Stacey at a vulnerable time in her life. We had a one-night stand. Who knows? Maybe it was a bad mistake.

And here I was at Grand Central terminal, the cathedral of mass transportation, talking to a smart and wonderful girl under the mural of stars as I waited to be slotted into the next train to Fordingtonville, still thinking of the ruins of my past with Stacey.

My answer to Kelly's question was, "I thought going to the city would be fun before I left."

"But are you having fun?"

I smiled and said, "I am."

There was a moment while we just sat and didn't say a word, just us and the echo of voices, voices I did not know.

There were millions of people in the city, passing one another, and here I met the one. And as I looked at the clock above the information booth, her train would be leaving in fifteen minutes.

In two days, we would be roughly three thousand miles apart, separated by a bunch of states that probably all had the same fast-food restaurants, the same gas stations, the same churches, the same bars, and probably the same conversations. All of these people between us, and fifteen minutes remained.

I grabbed her hand as our fingers laced. Her hand was smooth and soft.

We held hands and did not say a word for fifteen minutes. It was a risk, just like when I tried crossing Route 32 on my new bike. There was no looking both ways with Kelly. We connected. But the timing was not meant be.

Milky and Laura were approaching in the distance.

I let go of her hand.

We stood to greet them.

"So, here's the plan," Milky said. "I am gonna head back with Laura to Connecticut."

"For real?"

"Yeah. Can you take the truck back to your house and I'll stop by to get it later."

He handed me the keys to his beloved truck and whispered: "Don't worry, you'll see her again. I promise." He then hugged me—something he's never done. "I'm going to miss you."

***

I walked with Milky, Laura and Kelly to the train. Before Milky boarded, he hollered, "Don't crash my fucking truck." He then waved goodbye.

I turned to Kelly who had sad eyes. "Strange things can happen in one night."

"They sure can," I said.

"Good luck in film school."

Kelly hugged me.

I couldn't say anything.

I watched all three of them through the tinted windows looking for a seat. Milky and Laura sat together, and Kelly sat alone.

Not long after, the train began to move.

Kelly looked at me through the window and waved goodbye.

And within a few minutes, I was by myself.

CHAPTER 12

Black as Ink

I had nothing to read, and all the shops were closed. I sat by the payphones not far from the information booth, listening to people talk. I heard nothing interesting just, "yeah, I made it on time," "the food on the train tasted like garbage," "let me talk to mommy." I then tried counting the number of square tiles that extended to the information booth. That got boring real fast. I even timed how long it would take for this suit and tie guy to cart his luggage across the concourse.

I looked up at the timetable and saw the numbers flip for Hartford. I puckered my mouth and then pulled my legs to my chest.

I couldn't get her off my mind. I kept hearing Milky say, "Don't worry, man, you'll see her again."

I felt compelled to buy a ticket to Hartford and surprise them. We could go to the diner, talk about Kelly's piano class this fall. Milky could put his arm around Laura and say how he fucked up the radio interview for Dead and Gone.

I looked up at the timetable again. The Connecticut and Hudson lines departed around ten.

I stuck my hand down my sock and pulled out my sweaty train ticket.

Out of all of my friends, Milky was the one I trusted most. I would have stayed on the toboggan with Milky if I was there that snowy day. He wouldn't lie to me.

I stood.

Before leaving the concourse, I took one last look at the mural and all the constellations. Ships used to use the stars to navigate, and all I needed was this stamped piece of paper to go home.

I boarded the train.

A few people were reading, some sleeping, some staring into nowhere.

Over the humming of the train and the air conditioner was a voice that said: "This is the Hudson line."

The voice went on to say all the stops that the train would make, and one of those stops was Fordingtonville.

The train jolted, then began to move. The lights from the platform faded as the train headed into the abyss.

The darkness was like the Plaza's parking lot, the tundra, the nothingness.

I stared at my reflection in the window. I had not seen my face since the last time I was on the train. I looked tired, my hair was dry and frizzy from the humidity, and my eyes were drowsy.

I placed my hand on my reflection. I was going home and would soon leave New York.

The city's neon lights broke my reflection as the train blasted out of the abyss, now moving through the heart of Harlem.

The voice over the train's loudspeaker interrupted the flow. "Next stop, a Hundred and Twenty Fifth Street."

The train slowed to a halt.

The section of the train I was sitting in stopped at an overpass.

I could see the red neon lights read "Apollo," the crawl of car headlights, the routine of the traffic lights, and the people pounding the concrete.

The train started to move.

Gliding along, I observed the graffiti tagged on an old building. The characterized letters were illuminated by the dim color of streetlights.

We passed by a big oval bowl called YANKEE STADIUM.

Not long after the stadium, car headlights moved like a snake along the Major Deegan.

It wasn't long until the city lights slowly began to dissipate.

The moment of meeting Kelly, seeing Milky taking a chance with Laura, and Stacey leaving me on the Bowery were now memories.

Soon, the train headed under the Tappan Zee Bridge. From here on, it was nothing but suburbia. I closed my eyes and fell asleep.

A voice say we had arrived at Fordingtonville. I opened my eyes and saw the train parking lot.

Stepping off the train, I was greeted by the murky upstate air and the sound of crickets. I walked to Milky's truck, parked under the streetlight. In the distance, I could see the headlights from cars and trucks zooming along the Burghville-Fordingtonville Bridge.

I dug the keys out of my shorts and unlocked the door.

As I got behind the wheel, the seats were sticky from roasting in the sun all afternoon.

I started the truck and put the truck into first gear and headed out onto the highway, to quote the awesome metal band, Judas Priest.

Driving on Route 9, I moved northward toward the bridge.

Not long after, I reached the light for the bridge. I put on blinker, made a left turn, heading down the ramp, then merged onto Interstate 84.

Across the river, I smiled to see the blinking lights on the water tower.

I lit a cigarette and turned on the radio. I caught the beginning of The Who's "Reign oe'r Me."

The bridge was empty as I zoomed along with the song's soft piano intro.

As I reached the halfway mark of the bridge, Roger Daltrey's voice rumbled out of the speakers and into my soul. I must have heard the song a thousand times, but tonight there was something fresh about it.

I downshifted as I reached the exit for Burghville. I made a left at the light and then made a turn onto Powel Drive, next stop, Twilight Drive, where I lived.

I parked the car along the street. I did not want to block my mother or father's car in the driveway. The last thing I needed was someone to wake me up early and ask me to move a strange looking truck. I killed the engine and headed inside.

I entered my room and took off my sweaty and smelly shirt.

I sat on the corner of my bed and rubbed my eyes. I then turned on the fan.

After I turned off the lights. I laid down on the bed and stared at the blinking beacon lights on the water tower.

My heart was pumping fast. Man, I needed to quit smoking. I listened to the crickets and the squall of tires along Interstate 84, drowning out the ringing in my ears.

And for a moment, I was a part of the squall sound tonight.

CHAPTER 13

An Occurrence in the Vestibule (*reprise*)

It was Sunday, and the heat had not let up. I finished most of my packing around noon.

The week before, I had mailed my word processor, radio, CDs and cassettes to California to avoid the risk of the airline losing them.

My parents had a little party for me. My older brother and his wife came down from Vermont. He brought me a pack of condoms and some tips about California. He complained about my cigarette smoking, and even said he would send me some x-rays of cancer patients to scare me. I told him I was immortal.

My sister was there, too; she never left Burghville. She got a job at the bank and met some creditor named Gary who played in a jazz-blues band. Gary tried telling me what was wrong with the music I liked and that I should focus on the classics.

Anyway, the party ended around six or so. I had not heard from any of my friends.

It had been roughly ten hours since I had smoked a cigarette, and I was buzzing.

My brother and my father were doing the doctor talk when I decided to walk to The Plaza to buy some cigs. I could have taken Milky's truck, but I wanted to walk.

I reached the Tundra and headed through the parking lot to the big W. To my surprise, I saw Handsome and Russo sitting on the bench. "Hey!" I shouted.

Russo looked up at me with angry eyes.

"What the fuck happened to you guys last night?" I asked.

Russo stood and got in my face. "What the fuck happened to us?" He jabbed his index finger near my eyes and said, "What the fuck happened to you?!"

"What the hell is the matter with you?"

"You left us high and dry," Russo snapped.

"We couldn't find you," I said.

Russo shoved me. "Why did you persuade Milky to quit the band?"

That took me by surprise. "You talked to Milky?"

"He called me this afternoon and said he's picking up his gear. He quit the fucking band!"

Handsome got up. "Why did you leave us?"

"Milky got into a fight with some punk rockers. Next thing you know, we were walking the streets of Soho."

Russo stepped back from my space. He sat on the bench, and he blanketed his face with his hands.

I looked at Handsome. "Why didn't you wait for us to get back from the store?"

"Stacey got us backstage with F.U. We were going to get you and Milky to come back and meet everyone, but you guys were already gone," Handsome said. "It all happened so fast."

"No way!" I said.

"Yeah, it was nothing big," Russo said. "Backstage was small and it smelled like urine."

"How did you get home?"

"We rode back with F.U.," Russo dejectedly said.

In the background I heard a car ripping tire on The Tundra's skin. It sounded familiar. "I had nothing to do with Milky's decision. You know he was not happy with the band."

"The band is over," Russo said with downcast eyes.

"I don't know what to say. Start another band. Don't give up."

"Why do you care? You're leaving."

"Is this what it's all about?"

Russo chuckled, shaking his head. "No, Jimmy. I'm very happy for you," he said calmly. "I didn't mean to blame this on you. I'm sorry."

"It will be alright," I said.

I heard more tires screeching.

"I didn't mean to flip out on you," Russo said. "Fucking, Milky."

I laughed. "I gotta get some smokes. I'm dying for nicotine."

I entered the big W and strolled over to the record section. There was a small display for the new Jane's Addiction CD *Ritual De Lo Habitual*.

I thought about the entertainment buyer for the big W— this person must have good taste in music. Who knows? Maybe the buyer had dreams of working for a big record company and somehow things just didn't work out.

I grabbed the CD. The cover was pretty cool. It featured a red clay figure of a guy with his arms around two naked clay figured women. I liked what Milky had played for me. So I decided to take a chance. Besides, I needed a change, something new to listen to that wasn't metal or hardcore.

I walked to the counter and was surprised to see Loretta. I paid for the CD and got some change.

In the distance, I heard more tires screeching. With my quarters and my new CD, I entered the vestibule.

I injected the fresh quarters into the coin slot. I pulled the lever.

Nothing.

I pulled the lever again.

Still nothing.

I banged on the machine. "For Christ's sake!"

I kicked the machine. Then I heard a car engine. As the noise grew, I saw Russo and Handsome with fisheyes running toward me. They looked off at something, and then back to me, frantically waving for me to move.

My eyes nearly fell out of my head as I saw James Lebleau's Trans Am speeding toward the vestibule.

I bolted back into the store and then dived onto the floor. As I shielded my body, the Trans Am crashed through the vestibule, smashing into the cigarette and gumball machines.

I closed my eyes as shattered glass and debris rained down on me.

As the last piece of debris and glass fell to the ground, I opened my eyes, looking at the checkered blue tiled floor. Little blue, red, green and white gumballs rolled past me, freed from their domed existence in the gumball machine.

I couldn't hear anything as I laid on the floor.

Then I heard faint voices. The voices got clearer until I heard, "Bailey, you okay?" It was Russo's voice

I slowly leaned up and tried to look through the car's black tinted windows. I couldn't see anything inside. I could only hear the muffled sounds of the radio within the car. It was a metal band I had never heard.

I slowly pushed myself off the floor, trying not to slice myself on the shards of glass.

I lifted my left arm to make sure nothing was fractured. I was okay. I crept closer to the Trans Am and saw the nose of the car was planted halfway into the store, while the other half remained in the vestibule.

The cigarette machine rested askew on top of the hood, covering most of the front window.

The gumball machine, now residing in the record aisle, looked as if it had been shot out of a canon.

I saw Russo and Handsome moving slowly toward the destroyed vestibule.

Russo turned to Handsome. "Call an ambulance!"

Handsome ran to the payphone and then ran back. "I have no money!"

I approached the tinted window on the driver's side. I slowly moved my hand toward the door handle. It was locked. I looked through the dark window but could only see my own shadow looking back at me.

"James," I mumbled.

In the distance, I heard the faint sound of sirens. I sat on the floor.

My hands were shaking.

CHAPTER 14

Into The Twilight

My parents, Russo, Handsome and I stood in a circle at Departures. Not that we knew we were standing in a circle, but it was almost symbolic that we had formed one. But I knew in a few minutes I was ready to break free. Break away from my hometown, my family and friends.

Milky had called me that morning to wish me luck. He mentioned that Kelly was asking about me. I told him about James LeBleau and that I decided to quit smoking. He said it was a good idea and thought smoking was a cliché. I told him never to do an interview again.

When they announced that my plane would be boarding soon, my mother began to tear up. For a moment, I thought Russo and Handsome were about to cry. "Hey, I'll be home for Christmas," I said.

Russo hugged me and said, "Stay away from those porn actresses."

Handsome hugged me. "If you meet Nicole Kidman, drop her my number."

I kissed my mother, shook my father's sweaty hand, and then headed to the terminal.

I checked with the woman at the booth near the entrance. She said the plane would be half full and I may even have three seats to myself.

I sat down and rummaged through my bag to make sure I brought my Walkman.

Over the loudspeaker, a voice said, "Flight 122 to Chicago will be boarding in five minutes."

A line formed at the entrance.

I got up and grabbed my bag.

As I was walking to the line, I heard someone yell, "Jimmy!"

I looked back to see Stacey. She was wearing her father's motorcycle jacket. She ran to me as I dropped my bag.

She hugged me. "Please don't go," she cried.

"What's wrong?" I asked.

"I'm sorry, Jimmy. I am so sorry."

"I don't understand."

"Please stay. Don't leave."

I still had some time as we sat at the boarding area.

"I don't want you to be mad at me. I never meant to hurt you," she said.

"You mean about the city?"

"What you heard from Handsome is not true. I would never do anything like that. You know me, Jimmy. I'm not like that."

I nodded, then said. "I know."

I thought about the night Stacey and I shared in the parking lot at the Cathedral back in April.

I never told anyone about what happened between us. I had lied to Russo and the rest of the group about my sudden departure from the show. I had only missed Paine in the Neck's performance.

But when you were always hanging out with the same group of friends, and everyone knows everyone else's business, anything out of the ordinary was called into question. But no one had ever made the connection between me and Stacey. It was our secret.

I reached into my pocket and pulled out the postcard of Burghville that I bought in Soho. I handed it to her.

She took the card from me. "What's this?"

"Memories," I said.

I heard the last call to board my flight.

I caressed her leather jacket. "It's still too big for you."

She chuckled.

I kissed her on the forehead and then hugged her.

I grabbed my bag and then headed toward the flight attendant.

After she looked at my ticket, she smiled at me. "Have a nice flight."

Just before I entered the boarding bridge, I looked back.

Stacey she was gone.

I turned and walked down the bridge, crossing into the unknown. I wondered if I would ever see her again.

On the plane, I had all three seats to myself. I grabbed the Walkman out of my bag and sat by the window.

The sun had already set as an orange and yellow hue layered the western horizon.

The air tractor backed the airplane out of the terminal.

Not long after, the captain said over the intercom that it was a gorgeous night for flying and anticipated a smooth flight.

I watched the blue lights that went into the perspective point along the runway.

The nose of the plane stopped as we faced west. The engines began to roar as the plane quickly accelerated down the runway.

Suddenly, the plane began to lift.

Through the small window, I watched the earth tilt as we climbed the sky.

Within a few minutes, I flew over the water tower. Even though I could not see them, I knew my friends were down below, waving goodbye to me.

The plane swirled around the tower.

I looked back, watching the beacon lights blink on and off, on and off, and on and off.

Soon, the red lights of the tower faded away.

Once we hit cruising altitude, the red seatbelt light switched off.

The captain's voice came over the intercom and said it was okay to move around the cabin.

I stretched my legs and arms.

Listening to the white noise of the engines, I began to feel drowsy.

I put my headphones on and then closed my eyes.

I was running free.